United By The Moon Stalkers

By
Brook Winter

Table of Contents

Prologue

"Come on, this way," a voice in the shadows whispered out, gesturing his hand in a motion, as they understood immediately, slithering right after him in a quiet and barely noticeable motion, blending with the bushes and darkness.

It was a pretty normal and beautiful night in the lands of the Avronia's.

The beauty of the land was indubitable and unmatched, the twinkling stars of the night gave a magical glow to the land, and the wind gently caressed the land with its cool touch as it softly swayed the plants that grew along the land.

The moon hung majestically, casting an ethereal illumination on everything around it.

All was still, except for the sound of crickets that were chirping beautifully.

Avronia could be described as perfect. Magical even, filled with magnificence, glamor, and creatures that might blow your mind.

Well, except for the fact that this night, there were stalkers at the outskirts, watching, calculating, and their eyes intensely trained on the castle before them.

Sleek as the shadows, the figures prowled around in the darkness, keeping themselves hidden from view.

Their faces obscured by their signatory hoods and masks.

Their long black cloaks covered their body entirely. They were known to be stealthy like a ninja and silent like snakes. Their movements were smooth like water flowing, their weapons steadily strapped on their body like a second skin.

They blended into the shadows so seamlessly that it was impossible to distinguish their figure.

They were no other than the moon stalkers.

The most dreaded hunters of the werewolves.

The kingdom of Avronia was a land in which almost all supernatural creatures lived, and they all did in harmony.

The werewolves, to the witches, and any other supernatural.

Only that, each had their side of the land, which was divided by a thin magical wall.

The moon stalkers were only after the werewolves, which have been their sworn enemies from a long time.

"This way." Their leader gestured again, leading them through a large bush that led to the werewolves' castle.

They knew how alert the werewolves could be, so they had to act smarter and stealthier than usual.

The ambush was already moving in a smooth motion for them.

The leader of the moon stalkers kept himself hidden as he snuck closer to the castle, his eyes on the guard posts around the castle, where a few werewolves patrolled constantly.

He carefully pulled out his bow and arrow, deeply laced with wolfsbane, taking a step forward.

The others silently followed suit. He aimed the arrow and then silently let go, hitting one of the werewolves right on his chest.

He fell back and slumped over on the ground, dead instantly.

The other stalkers began firing arrows toward other guards, silently killing them, while he made his move.

He dashed towards the open gate and shot another wolf down, making quick work of it.

The others followed closely behind him, silently killing the few remaining guards, save one, who had narrowly escaped and made a run into the castle to alert the rest.

"Shit!" The leader exclaimed as he saw that they ran up straight into a pack of already-shifted wolves.

"Get ready for action. And this is unto death."

The leader said to the other members of the stalker's group, while the wolves growled at them, baring their sharp canines, as though awaiting a signal to pounce.

With swift movements, they all drew their bows and arrows, aiming them at the wolves. "Now!" They roared together, as they fired their arrows, while the wolves drew their claws, pouncing on them.

The two sides clashed and growled furiously at each other.

Blood, guts, and war.

The werewolf king roared and fought ferociously, trying to kill anyone within reach with his bare hands and teeth.

His eyes burned with anger as he struggled against the moon stalkers, none getting the upper hand, as both the dead bodies of the stalkers and the wolves were sprawled everywhere on the castle grounds.

***

Cadence felt something was not right, as she tossed and turned on her soft, silky bed, unable to sleep. She didn't understand why, but something did seem off.

She threw off the covers and got out of bed, slipping on a long white robe to cover up the flimsy silk dress she always wore to bed, before walking over to the window.

There, the moon was shining brightly outside her castle, with stars sprinkled across the sky.

It was almost the dawn of a new day.

Cadence stood there, looking down at the beautiful scenery of the Avronian kingdom, which was surrounded by hills and forests and fields filled with grasses.

Everything seemed perfect, but her mind raced a thousand miles, as she could feel that something was wrong somewhere.

Cadence looked around and couldn't find anything amiss. Everything appeared fine and peaceful, just like always.

She was about to retire back to her bed when her eyes caught a little movement by the boundary, which led to the wolves.

Her heart jumped a little at the sight. Something wasn't right.

With a deep sigh, Cadence closed her eyes and slowly waved her hand mid-air, causing the barrier she had created to begin depleting, in order to give her a clearer view of what was happening in the wolves' territory.

She gasped as her eyes flew open.

What greeted her was a bloodbath and fire outbreak in the werewolves' land.

A lot of corpses of wolves and a little of what seems to be likened to humans, lay strewn all over the place, some of them still alive, moaning in pain or struggling to get away.

"The moon stalkers," Cadence said with gritted teeth and fierce anger burning in her now red orbs, as realization dawned on her.

Asides being the most powerful witch in the whole of Avronia kingdom and probably the world at large, Cadence, had the power of keen eyesight and hearing whatever she needed to, despite the distance.

She was considered a goddess.

Her power could make people do her will, and her senses were unparalleled by anything and everything in the world.

Cadence took in a whole lungful of breath, shutting her eyes close, as she called out a spell that made her levitate over to the wolves' territory, where the war grew hotter.

She saw the battle from far above and felt an immense rage boiling up inside her, as she witnessed the carnage and mayhem.

She cursed loudly at the thought of the moon stalkers.

She watched the wolves fighting valiantly as they tried to defend the territory and defend themselves from the enemy.

Unable to watch it go on anymore, she let out a loud shriek of rage and released all the magic in her to stop the slaughter.

A blinding light burst forth, covering the battlefield, blinding everyone with its intensity and heat.

When the light died down and disappeared, everyone was unconscious, some dead.

Cadence felt the last streak of her magic leave her, as she had exerted everything just to save the werewolves. She felt her body grow weak, as she still hung in the air.

Slowly, she felt life seeping out of her, too weak to fight it anymore, she gave in, and her eyes closed shut, while she let herself get engulfed in darkness.

Chapter One

A thousand years later...

Silas paced around his room, trying to calm his nerves before he would appear before the king and queen of the kingdom.

It's been three days in a row, and his people who were guarding the kingdom's boundaries were slaughtered one by one.

All in the same pattern.

"Alpha." Came James, Silas's beta, a sullen look on his face, as he made his way into Silas's room.

"What's the current news? How is he doing?" Alpha Silas asked in urgency, as he met James halfway, asking about the last werewolf who was attacked during his parole at the boundary.

James sighed, his eyes downcast. "I'm sorry Alpha, but we lost him," Beta James said, his tone heavy with sorrow. "The pack doctor did all she could," he added. "The wounds were deep, three slashes across their chest. Silver blades dipped in wolfsbane. Literally impossible to escape death."

Silas's eyes widened, his breathing suddenly coming faster. "No," he murmured, his voice filled with shock. "It can't be true..." he trailed off, trying to make sense of the whole situation.

"I'm sorry, but it is," Beta James said with a grim expression.

"What about the trails of the attackers? What are they? Who are they?" Alpha Silas asked all at once.

Beta James let out a long, exasperated sigh. "I'm sorry, my alpha, but there was none. The assailants covered their tracks real good. There was nothing."

"Fuck!" Alpha Silas yelled out unexpectedly, kicking the first furniture his feet came in contact with, sending it in splitters everywhere in the room.

Silas closed his eyes tight for a second, taking in an even deeper breath, calming himself. When he opened his eyes again, he spoke slowly and carefully. "Thank you, Beta. I will go speak with the king and queen, and then see what else I can do. You should inform everyone else of this new development so they can be on their guard and highly alert, in case it happens again," Alpha Silas said quietly.

His beta gave a slight nod of his head in understanding. "Yes Alpha, I'll do just that." Beta James bent in a bow before turning and heading outside, closing the door behind him. Alpha Silas watched after him until he was sure the other man had left, then sank back onto the nearest couch, shaking his head in disbelief and rage at the loss of his people.

He needed to clear his head, before going to face the king and the queen of the kingdom.

Silas got back to his feet, running his hand through his raven black hair and pushing his bangs away from his forehead. His brown eyes were hard when he looked up, his shoulders pulled in a tense line.

"Calm down Silas. Take a deep breath," he said to himself, as he walked to his mirror, staring at his image. He could feel his wolf, Leo, at the surface, seeing his eyes flicker from their original brown color to gold.

The golden flecks grew to an almost iridescent color in a flash of silver, showing how agitated his wolf was, knowing exactly what Silas was feeling.

Silas ran his fingers through his hair again and sighed, letting it hang loose over his shoulders.

Leo growled slightly, causing Silas to glance at his reflection and give a small chuckle. "I know boy, I'm beyond pissed now, but we need to keep it under control," Silas said to his reflection, staring fiercely back at his image, which seemed like he had aged a little more than his twenty-eight old self, in the werewolf equivalent.

After another minute, he finally calmed down enough to put on a blank expression and walk out of his room, making his way down the hallway of his mansion, toward the main entrance.

"My keys," he said to his butler, stretching his hand out, as his strides were still quick and fast, while he walked toward his black 1965 Volvo P1800, the newest edition as of then.

"Here it is Alpha," the butler said breathlessly, handing over the car key to Silas.

"Have a good evening Alpha," he said in an overly bright tone, his voice sounding strained.

Silas turned his head to gaze briefly at his servant and nodded curtly at him. "Get my room fixed before I'm back," Silas instructed, before getting into the driver's side of his vehicle. He slammed the door shut, and the engine roared to life immediately. The car lurched forward, moving quickly down the driveway and towards town.

The land of Avronia was purely a realm of the supernatural, but with time, most of the supernaturals got to mate with humans from the human realm, bringing them in here.

The car sped through the streets of his capital city at inhuman speed, the sun starting to set below the horizon. It was late in the day, the sky painted purple and pink, as the last rays of sunlight shone on the darkening forest surrounding the city.

It was silent in the car for the majority of the drive, only broken occasionally by the sound of his radio playing the latest hits from his favorite bands.

The music filled the car, soothing Silas, with a sense of peace. His anger, frustration, and anxiety, disappeared for a moment.

As the car neared the outskirts of Avronia's capital city, the roads became a little more crowded with cars and people.

More residential, with houses lining both sides of the street.

Silas swerved his car to a sharp bend that led to the castle of the King of Avronia.

He drove down the gravel drive until he arrived at the huge castle gate, which allowed no visitors inside except those with a Royal Seal of approval.

Silas rolled down the windows, as one of the royal guards made his way to him.

"Alpha Silas," he said with a courtesy nod, which was reciprocated by the Alpha.

"The King and Queen don't seem to be expecting you tonight," the guard said politely.

"Yes, I know. But it's a matter of urgency," Alpha Silas responded, sick of the unnecessary protocol already.

"Of course, Alpha. Do let me make a quick call," the guard said, moving to the other side, while he spoke into his walkie-talkie.

After a few talks and responses in his talkie, he walked back to the alpha, who was mentally hanging on a thin line, really close to losing it.

"The King and Queen will have you," the royal guard said to the alpha, nodding to the two other guards who stood by the gate, instructing that they open up the gate.

Alpha Silas didn't waste a second driving in, once the gates flew open, parking right at the castle's entrance.

He got out of the car and strode up the front steps. The guard standing by the doors quickly approached him, opening his hands with a bow to get the Alpha's car keys in order to park his car in a better place.

Alpha Silas flung it to him, as he made his way with quick strides into the royal castle.

The interior of the castle was dim, but illuminated by torches lit throughout the large halls.

It was beautiful in its design, with marble floors and ornate walls, which were filled with pictures of past royals.

The stone walls glowed softly with soft light, giving the hallways an enchanting glow.

In the center of the castle stood a massive throne room. The ceiling soared high above them, depicting a giant eagle flying majestically.

Around the center of the throne room was a magnificent throne, adequately adorned with gold and sparkles of diamonds on it.

On top of the throne sat the King and Queen of Avronia. King Xavier and Queen Astrid, majestically settled on each of their throne seats.

They were dressed in matching white royal regal with intricate gold embroidery.

Queen Astrid wore her blonde hair in a sleek twist on the crown of her head, where her crown settled on beautifully, while her husband sported his signature silver hair underneath his crown, letting it flow at the nape of his neck, looking dashing and distinguished.

At the sight of Alpha Silas approaching the royal couple, the king stepped up and stood before his throne, awaiting the Alpha.

"Your majesty," Silas said with a bow, as he got to the throne step.

"Alpha Silas! Still ravishing as ever!" The king exclaimed, pulling up Silas back to his feet, as he gave him a warm bear hug.

Queen Astrid stepped forward and hugged Silas tightly as well, holding his head gently between her hands as she placed a kiss on his temple.

"What brings you here child, you seem disturbed?" she asked, her voice full of concern as she held him close to her, searching his eyes.

Silas sighed and shook his head. "My pack has been under attack for the past few days, we've lost three werewolves already, and my people aren't safe," Silas stated all at once, pulling back from the Queen's grip.

Queen Astrid frowned worriedly, while the King looked shocked, his eyebrows furrowing together at the Alpha's words. "A pack attacked your people? Who would dare do such a thing!"

"It wasn't a werewolf or a rogue attack. It was something else, I don't know what they are, but I know they are very powerful and extremely dangerous," Alpha Silas said silently, as both the King and Queen returned to their former positions on the throne.

They both looked thoughtful, as if they were trying to come up with a plan.

"You say you have no idea whatsoever of what they look like?" the king asked, once again, stroking his chin thoughtfully.

"Yes. But their killings were precise and calculated. Three deep stripes of deep cuts on the chest, with silver blades, deeply laced with wolfsbane, and no trail or track left behind. Whoever they might be, they are incredibly skilled, which is why we're having a hard time tracking them," Silas replied.

King Xavier's face paled for a moment, as Silas let in the details, but immediately concealed it.

There was a stretch of awkward silence for a short while, as everyone was lost in thinking.

King Xavier broke the silence first. "Did any werewolves manage to survive to tell you anything about this?" he asked slowly.

"None survived. Sadly, they were either killed on the spot or didn't make it before getting to the pack's doctor, as they lost lots of blood to the fact that the silver and wolfsbane prevented them from healing quick enough. The last die due to blood shortage," Alpha Silas quickly explained.

The King's face remained impassive, as the gears began turning in his head, before he spoke again, speaking slowly and carefully as he did so.

"These attackers are most definitely from the supernatural," The king said thoughtfully. "So what would you want to do about it?" the king asked Alpha Silas, who already had his thinking gears rolling.

"I think we should contact the other werewolf packs in Avronia, see if any are willing to aid in a battle against these creatures. If not...," Silas trailed off, still thinking, "Then I'm afraid we'll have to resort to magic. This is an extreme situation, and a slippery one too. We need to get ahead of whoever is behind this," Silas said.

The King nodded along, looking deep in thought as he contemplated what to do next. "I'll put out an urgent call to all packs in Avronia, just to see what we can gather, so that we have a fighting chance," he said, skipping out the second option.

"But don't you think using magic would be more effective?" Alpha Silas asked, his eyes trained on the king.

"We do not possess magic Alpha Silas, so where in the name of the moon goddess do you seek to gain magic from?" the King said a little too forcefully.

"From what I can recall from the legend of Avronia." Alpha Silas began, slowly pacing before the thrones. "A witch named Cadence saved our people from the moon stalkers. This could be a similar case," Alpha Silas said, stroking his chin, as he came to an abrupt stop. "Something in my gut tells me the witch is still alive, and we can find her. I mean, there was no record of her body found anywhere after the Great War," Alpha Silas said, oblivious to the fact that the king had started burning to a certain emotion while the Queen shifted uncomfortably in her seat.

"Yes, that is it!" Alpha Silas suddenly exclaimed, pulling his attention back to the king.

"King Xavier, I do plead for your permission to seek for the old witch Cadence, in order to save my people."

Chapter Two

The chirping birds by her window woke Blair up. She opened her eyes to a sunny morning, stretching on her bed, with a loud yawn. Sunlight filtered through the curtains in an inviting fashion. She didn't want to move from her comfortable bed, but she knew she had a long day ahead of her.

Blair's stomach grumbled in protest. She would have much preferred to sleep in a little longer before she got her day started. However, it was time to get up.

She stretched, then climbed out of bed, and walked to her windows, pushing them fully open.

"Good morning, my neighbors!" Blair yelled out with her face out the window, smiling as the morning air gently brushed against her cheeks.

"Shut the fuck up!" A deep voice down below replied.

"Do have a lovely day too!" She yelled back, laughing alongside. She was still not going to get over this. It was most definitely the highlight of her mornings.

Blair pulled back from her window, with a twirl, feeling like one of the fairy tale princesses, with her hair flowing around her shoulders and her golden curls glinting in the sunshine.

She made her way to her little kitchen and carried on with her usual morning routine.

As usual, she prepared herself for a nice cup of coffee and waited for it to brew. Her favorite mug sat by the counter, next to the book she had been so engrossed in for the past few days now.

As soon as her kettle whistled, indicating her coffee was ready, she poured herself a cup and took it to the living room alongside her book.

Call her old-fashioned, but she loved starting her day with a cup of coffee, black with no sugar or cream, exactly how she loved it.

She settled into her armchair, flipping the pages of her book until she got to the page she was last at.

With the tip of her thumb, she traced along the edge of her coffee cup before raising it to her lips, for a long sip from it.

She closed her eyes and breathed deeply, as she pulled the cup back from her lips.

The scent calmed her soul, soothing her senses that always seemed alert when they needed rest.

She leaned back on her armrest chair, placing the cup back on the table, sighing deeply, as she let her mind drift.

This was always the best part of her morning, where she got to meditate and let her mind relax.

It was so peaceful. So serene.

The sound of the morning breeze caressing the leaves above her roof, lulling her to sleep yet again.

****

She was back to where she had first woken up after a long time.

Her body battered, her throat scratchy from lack of water and food, and her hair matted together in dried cakey mud.

The mud caked also under her nails and stuck to her clothes. She had no idea whatsoever, of where she was.

Her breath came heavily in heavy pants as she struggled to keep herself standing upright.

The sun was setting.

She began walking forward, ignoring the burning pain that burned all through her limbs, staring at the vast deciduous land, stretching as far as the eye could see.

She was lost in the middle of nowhere.

Her memories and magic lost.

Her body slowly gave out, her arms weak and tired from struggling with every step she took, each inhale sending waves of pain through her torso.

Her sight of vision slowly became blurry as the world tilted around her.

Her legs gave in, causing her to buckle beneath her, falling onto her knees.

She cried out as the dirt and rocks dug painfully into her knees. She tried to pull herself back up to her feet again, but the effort sent her crashing back down, her hands grabbing desperately at the soil for dear life.

Her lungs were on fire, she couldn't breathe.

She looked up.

The evening sun shone harshly on her, casting its golden rays, and causing the sweat which flowed from her forehead to glint under its glare.

She gasped for some air, her chest constricted painfully from trying so hard, as she felt herself slowly slipping into darkness again.

"No..." She managed out, as her body fell limply on the dried mud, her eyes slowly shutting close.

She couldn't fight anymore, there was nothing left for her, nothing left but darkness.

"That's someone there!" She heard a voice call out, or had she imagined it?

"She's still alive!" Another voice said, but closer now, crouching right beside her.

Her eyes slowly fluttered open, making out faint figures which came close to her, before she finally shut her eyes again and gave into darkness yet again.

***

A loud bang on Blair's door brought her back from her short nap, making her jerk upright on her seat, confusion deeply furrowed in her brows, as she blinked furiously, trying to make sense of where she was.

"Blair!" A voice called out from the other side of her door, jolting her back to reality.

"Oh my." She sighed out, realizing she was back in her house, she quickly got onto her feet, her book sauntering to the floor simultaneously.

There was another pounding on the door, louder than before.

"Coming! I'm coming!" She yelled, rubbing the sleep away from her eyes. As she opened the door, there stood, Jemima, her palace source, covered in a huge cloak.

"The royal guards are lurking around this corner," Jemima said, pushing her way past Blair, to get into her apartment.

Blair stared at both sides of her passageway, seeing no one, she shrugged and got in, shutting her door afterward.

"Are you okay? You look like hell," Jemima said, plowing down on one of the couches, picking up the book Blair had been reading to stare at the covers.

"There are no pictures in that," Blair said with a smile, as she sat back on her armrest chair, her eyes on Jemima.

"Urgh. Boring," Jemima said, pulling out her tongue in a dramatic way, dropping back the book on the table. "I'm starving! What do you have prepared?" she said, getting off the couch, and made her way to the kitchen.

"Oh my," Blair said, as she got to her feet too. "I haven't made anything. I just realized I haven't had my breakfast either. What time is it?" She looked over the grandfather wall clock, which hung at a side in her living room.

"Oh my, it's noon already." Blair rushed into her kitchen to see Jemima stuff her face with crackers from the can.

"You must be hungry then, because I am famished. Let me get something for us to eat." Blair went to the cabinet, taking out some ingredients she had put there earlier in the week.

She grabbed the pasta and eggs while rummaging through the fridge, for anything else she needed to make something delicious.

She pulled out some cheese from her drawer, while Jemima helped her by gathering the necessary herbs to prepare her dish.

Soon the two women were busy stirring the pot with the saucepan that Blair had just heated up.

Once the mixture was ready, Blair scooped a bit of it in a spoon, and passed it to Jemima. The smell of lasagna wafting towards her nostrils made her mouth water even though her stomach was rumbling for sustenance.

Jemima eagerly shoved a fork full of the mixture into her mouth, moaning loudly, causing Blair to chuckle in amusement.

"Wow. That's really good," Jemima mumbled through her mouthful of food, after she had swallowed it and was able to speak again.

"Thank you. I thought it would taste better than toast," Blair commented, as she placed the pan into the oven, waiting for the lasagna to finish cooking.

"Good choice though," Jemima said, taking a seat on one of the stools in the kitchen.

After the pasta was done cooking, Blair took the pan and served the pieces of lasagna on two separate plates for both Jemima and herself.

Blair watched how Jemima dug in without any hesitation.

She loved how much the young girl trusted her, and she wished she could do more for her, but at the moment, there was absolutely nothing she could do for her.

Jemima was not only a slow bloomer, but the least of the werewolf chain, an omega.

Most omegas where treated with less regard in the wolves' realm. Most were made to be slaves, serving in the royal palace, while some, especially the females, were given out as mistresses to some of the alphas and betas in the land.

Blair found Jemima on the street, beaten and battered. Unable to leave the young girl who seemed to be around her late teen years alone and cold on the street, she picked her up, nursed her wounds, fed her, bringing her back to life literally.

She got to learn that Jemima was the target of bullies in her school and anywhere she found herself, because she was a slow bloomer.

Jemima never got to shift till she was twenty when her wolf finally surfaced.

Blair managed to get Jemima to the palace to work in the kitchen, through the help of an old friend, as she couldn't get to take care of her as her own, since she had not the resources and she also didn't want the attention being drawn to her.

In return, Jemima worked hard for Blair, bringing all sources of information she could gather from the palace back to her.

"Thank you so much Blair," Jemima said, clearing the last of her plate.

"And to think you work in the kitchen." Blair let out a short chuckle, slowly stuffing her food into her mouth, while she watched Jemima. Her appetite seemed to never end.

"So..." Blair started, picking up the now empty dishes and loading them in the sink to wash them.

"Any news from the palace?" Blair asked, turning on the tap to let the water run on the dishes.

"Nothing interesting. Same political stuffs, blah blah," Jemima said, stretching on her chair in a dramatic way.

Blair chuckled to herself, nodding in understanding, as she kept doing the dishes.

"So nothing at all? No visit from strange faces, nothing has been amiss?" Blair asked, rinsing off the foam from the dishes under the running water, before gently placing them back in the cupboard.

"About visits..." Jemima trailed, as though trying to recall a piece of this particular information. "Alpha Silas of the silver claw pack came visiting the king and queen unannounced," she said, gaining Blair's attention now.

"I think I had a glimpse of him, and damn, Alpha Silas's beauty is to die for!" Jemima exclaimed in a day dreamy voice.

"How do I even deal?" Blair rolled her eyes, wiping her hand on her dress, as she turned back to face Jemima.

"And what did he come here for? Is there anything about our kingdom he wanted to know?"

Blair asked all at once, wondering why an Alpha would come around on short notice without the invitation from the king and queen.

"He did look distressed, though, but it seem to be all about his pack." Jemima shrugged.

"Hmm..." Blair hummed, her mind gaining interest in what the alpha might have come around for, and the silver claw was located at the outskirts of Avronia, close to the boundaries.

"Yeah, I can remember something." Jemima suddenly pipped, gaining Blair's attention fully again.

"I heard him say something about war, magic, a legend probably, and he ended it with seeking permission to go search for a particular witch to help them." Jemima shrugged.

"A witch?" Blair repeated, her attention fully on Jemima now.

"Yeah… and I think he mentioned her name," Jemima said, still deep in thoughts.

"Okay?" Blair asked, urging her to continue.

"He said, they need to find a witch by the name Cadence," Jemima said, not aware of the pale expression that graced the face of Blair, who looked like she had just seen a ghost.

Chapter Three

"King Xavier, I do plead for your permission to seek for the old witch Cadence, in order to save my people," Alpha Silas said, his head held up high, as he felt confident enough that his request would be considered by the king.

There was a short moment of silence.

"Alpha Silas," King Xavier said finally, after letting out a deep long sigh. "You are one of the best Alphas the land of Avronia has been gifted with, no doubt. But this request you've made, is one which, as much as I'd love to give a go-ahead to, I'm extremely sorry, Alpha Silas, but your request is declined," he said solemnly.

"King Xavier." Alpha Silas chuckled slowly, bowing his head a bit, before looking back to the king with an impassive expression. "I guess I didn't present my request in a rightful manner. I'm sorry," the Alpha said bowing again to the king. "Queen Astrid." He turned his attention to her, giving her a smile and a bow too, before returning his attention to the king.

"I humbly ask for your permission, not your men, or guards, no." He shook his head with yet another chuckle. "I need just your permission, a go-ahead, and I'll take up the rest myself. Find the witch and ask for help, and everyone is happy and settled. Simple," Alpha Silas said with a tight-lipped smile, looking at the King expectantly. He waited patiently.

"My answer remains no," King Xavier said without batting an eye.

"Seems like you still don't get me, King Xavier, with all due respect, actually," Alpha Silas said with another dry chuckle, as he paced a bit.

"I heard you loud and clear Alpha, and my answer still remains no!" The king exclaimed, clearly getting agitated now.

"Why?" Alpha Silas asked, clenching his fist by his side, as he tried to keep his anger in check.

"It's been years since she was last heard of."

Queen Astrid, who had been quiet for the whole ordeal, finally spoke up, as the tension in the throne room became a little tense. "About a thousand years ago. And the possibility of it being just a myth is valid. I mean, none of us got to meet her, all we heard were stories, the validity of it, not ascertained. So try to understand with the king that your request is impossible and for your greater good. What if you get hurt, or worse still something worse happens to you while you go in search of something that is nonexistent? Think about it, Alpha Silas," Queen Astrid said in a soothing voice.

"And what if you're wrong? What if she's alive, somewhere in this realm? I mean, there was no record of her death, and neither was it recorded that she was buried. How would we even know if a chance isn't given to find her?" Alpha Silas replied immediately, hope glinting in his eyes that he was having an upper hand already.

The Queen sighed as her face fell. "I tried, really." The Queen shook her head, leaning back on her throne seat.

"King Xavier," Alpha Silas said calmly as he turned back to the King. "I'm not asking for much." He let out a deep sigh. "Just your approval should in case I'll have to leave the borders," Alpha Silas said.

"My answer is no!" The king snapped out. "And you're not to make mention of this anymore, ever again! You'll be damned with the consequences if you ever do! And that's final!" The king exclaimed, staring directly at Alpha Silas, his eyes blaring.

"But, but your highness..." Alpha Silas tried protesting but was cut short by the king.

"No buts Silas! You may take your leave now," King Xavier said in a dismissive tone.

The two stared at each other, for several seconds, neither wanting to back down, while Queen Astrid had a pleading look in her eyes, directed to Alpha Silas, who she was sure was close to snapping out, as his eyes flickered from brown to golden yellow, and back to brown again.

With a deep sigh of defeat, Alpha Silas bowed, "Your majesty. The Queen," He said with gritted teeth before raising his head back up.

"Do have a lovely evening, you both," he said with a smile, as he rose his head back up. His eyes back to brown, indicating that he had gotten full control over Leo, who so badly wanted to surface.

With yet another bow, Alpha Silas made his way out of the throne room.

Once he got to the palace entrance, the guard to whom he had handed his keys stretched it out to him, his car back to the entrance.

"Thank you," Alpha Silas said to the guard, as he grabbed his keys in a quick motion and stalked to the driver's side of his car.

"Beta James," Alpha Silas called through his mind link channel, as he unlocked his car door and got inside.

"Alpha." Beta James's voice sounded in his head in no time.

"Get prepared. We are visiting the rogues soon," the alpha said through the mind link, turning on the ignition of his car.

"What- Yes sir!" Beta James said, his voice quivering.

"Have a problem with that?" Alpha Silas responded while he drove out of the palace grounds with a sudden speed, his voice a hint of aggression, as though daring the beta to protest.

"No... No Alpha," came the beta's voice almost immediately.

"Good," Alpha Silas said and shut out the mind link, once he got to the palace gates.

"Alpha." The royal guard who stood by the gate nodded, as he rolled the gate open, giving a slight bow to the alpha, as he made his way out.

Alpha Silas drove at the utmost speed his car could go, dangerously swerving and dodging cars in his path. His hands gripped his steering wheel so tightly that they began turning white, he was clearly agitated, as all he saw was red.

Leo so badly wanted to surface, break free, maybe cause a little havoc here and there before he could be satiated, but Alpha Silas wasn't having any of it. He knew acting up in that situation would only bring about more damage and probably a war breakout too.

In no time, Alpha Silas was back in his territory, his eyes fixed on the road. He stopped the car just in front of his mansion. His beta James, was already awaiting him at the entrance of the mansion.

"Alpha Silas, I reached out to the leader of the rogues, and he refused honoring our invite," Beta James said, bowing to the alpha, as he tried keeping up with the alpha's long strides into the mansion.

"Then we will go meet them," Alpha Silas said, still maintaining his pace toward his office in the mansion.

"Alpha? The rogues?" Beta Silas asked in shock, halting his steps back a bit.

"Did I stutter when I said we are going to meet them?" Alpha Silas asked, halting in his steps too, as he turned over to his beta, giving him a fierce look.

"I'm sorry, alpha." Beta James bowed his head, not daring to look back at the alpha who he knew was clearly furious.

"You should be," Alpha Silas said, as he picked back up his strides to the office, with his beta, right behind, trying his best to keep up with the alpha.

Alpha Silas walked to the large mahogany desk, as he got to it, he sat down behind it. He took out some files from one of the drawers and opened them up on his desk. He looked up to his beta, who stood by the entrance of his office. Beta James nodded.

"Send the order. We will move out today," Alpha Silas said, with a hard expression, as he put the files which were on his desk away.

"Yes, Alpha," Beta James replied with a bow.

"Meet at the mansion's entrance in ten," Alpha Silas said as he got to his feet, making his way to his office door.

"Duly noted alpha," Beta James confirmed.

With another nod from Alpha Silas, the beta left quickly, as Alpha Silas made his way back to his room.

His room was as sparkly as ever. Gone was the destroyed furniture, a new one had been immediately replaced.

Alpha Silas slowly paced around his room, his breathing labored, as he replayed the event of the day in his head.

"Fuck!" He growled out, clenching his fists and holding himself back from destroying yet another.

With a deep sigh, Alpha Silas made his way to his wine cellar in the room, pulling out a bottle of whiskey and a glass.

He poured himself some in a glass, and with a quick swig, he gulped down the whole content, letting the burning sensation consume his throat.

He held the glass midair, sighing out, before leaning forward to the wall before him, resting his head and closing his eyes for a few moments, trying to calm himself down with the alcohol.

After a couple of minutes, he stood up straight again, placed the bottle of whiskey back in the cellar, the glass on the counter and headed to the bathroom.

As Alpha Silas got to his bathroom, he headed straight for the sink, where he turned on the tap and splashed icy cold water on his face.

After a few seconds, he raised his head up to stare at his reflection on the mirror, which hung above the bathroom sink.

A frown graced his face, as he stared back at his own reflection.

The black-haired werewolf in the mirror had dark circles under his eye, and his hair was disheveled due to the number of times he ran his fingers through it.

He could hear his heart beating loudly against his ears, his chest rising faster with every breath. His eyes were glowing faintly, Leo begging to be released.

"Calm down boy, I'll get you out soon," he said with a soothing voice to his wolf, as he wiped his face with the towel which hung overhead.

"Let's do this," Alpha Silas said, feeling a bit calmer as he made his way out of the bathroom and headed straight to his wardrobe.

"Are you ready?" Alpha Silas mind linked with his beta, as he draped on a dark leather jacket over his shoulder.

"Yes, Alpha," Beta James responded immediately.

"Alright, see you in two," Alpha Silas said, quickly making his way back at the mansion's entrance.

"Let's go," Alpha Silas said, getting into the passenger's side of the car, letting Beta James get into the driver's side. He couldn't trust himself on the wheels at that moment.

They drove in silence towards the outskirts of his territory, where the rouges had pitched their den at the edge of the woods.

Alpha Silas instructed his beta to park the vehicle outside the woods, just near the center of a clearing they got to.

"What now?" the beta asked, as they both sat in silence, staring at the empty space before them.

"We wait," Alpha Silas responded, relaxing back on his chair rest, positive that the rogue leader was going to make his way to them soon, seeing they had infiltrated his territory.

The sun was setting, casting long shadows over everything.

Alpha Silas felt the tension between them rise to dangerous levels, as they waited, knowing full well what they were risking by coming to meet these people. But they couldn't stay away, they needed help, and the rogues were the last resort.

"What's taking him so long?" Beta James growled through clenched teeth, stretching his hand to the door when the alpha stopped him.

"Calm down James. They'll come around," Alpha Silas said in a quiet voice.

"But Alpha." Beta James tried protesting.

"Relax," Alpha Silas interrupted him, his tone stern. "Just relax."

Not long after, a figure appeared out of the darkness, making its way towards them, as the moonlight illuminated his figure.

It was the rogue leader. He was huge and menacing looking, with short, grey-colored hair, and a long scar which ran through his right piercing silver eyes.

"Well, well, well... if it isn't Alpha Silas and his beta," The rogue leader said as Alpha Silas and Beta James got out of the vehicle. "To what do I owe the pleasure?" the rogue leader said sarcastically, as Alpha Silas approached him.

"I need your help." Alpha Silas deadpanned, fully aware of the fact that they were surrounded.

Chapter Four

Blair tightened the cloak which was over her head, as she walked by the sidewalk of the city's road.

In all honesty, she wasn't quite sure where she was going, but she wanted to walk for a bit, breathe in some fresh new air, see the city, and return back to the comfort of her home.

The cold wind bit at her nose, causing a shiver to run down her body, causing her hands to tremble.

Okay, maybe not this type of air.

Blair pulled the cloak more firmly around herself with both hands as she stared forward again, looking straight ahead.

In no time, Blair found herself in the city's park, walking on one of its paths.

It seemed almost peaceful, even though there weren't many people around, just a couple of children playing in the snow, their parents chatting and drinking coffee while watching the kids play.

A dog barked from somewhere nearby, probably someone having trouble controlling his dog.

She took in a deep breath, before letting it out in a sigh.

The cold winter air felt so nice. And Blair was glad that she had dressed warmly enough. She had, under her cloak, an old pair of jeans and her sweater. The boots on her feet were also very thick.

The sound of leaves rustling brought her attention back to the present.

"Hey! Watch it!" Blair yelled as she was rudely bumped into.

"You-" She paused halfway, placing her raised finger back to her side, on seeing she was bumped by one of the royal soldiers, who turned over to look at her with a scowl on his face.

"Sorry. Uh, excuse me," Blair mumbled. He didn't say anything back, only gave her a quick nod and turned on his heel, joining the rest of the guards who headed to a particular huge tree at the center of the park.

Blair frowned, she wondered what exactly the royal guards wanted there and at that point.

She narrowed her eyes as she watched the six royal guards stand before the tree, as one of them pulled out a piece of paper that seemed like it had inscriptions on it, a picture maybe, but it was too far for even her squinted eyes to grasp.

She watched them paste the paper on the tree trunk and then immediately started moving, making their way to another location.

As soon as they left, Blair's curiosity got the better of her.

Without any second thought, she marched towards the tree, stopping right before the poster.

"Wanted! Dead or Alive, notorious badmen. Hmm, interesting," she said with renewed interest, staring at the picture of two men, one of which gave out the aura of a leader, an alpha maybe, and the other looked equally dangerous but in a roguish way, and a young woman with blonde hair, cut short in a bob, and could easily be mistaken to be the opposite gender from her choice of dressing.

"The following members of a new gang, led by a werewolf Alpha, Alpha Silas, are wanted by the king, for starting up unrest in the land of Avronia, by starting up a search of the nonexistent witch Cadence..." Blair trailed off, her lips curving downwards. This was news indeed, she thought with keen interest.

"Causing panic in the land. If found, report to the royal palace immediately, a whopping reward awaits them," Blair read. Her eyebrow rose as she heard the last sentence.

"Alpha Silas..." she said in almost a whisper, as her hand trailed on the part of the poster which had the Alpha's face on it. "What do you want Cadence for?" she wondered, still staring at the dangerously handsome alpha on the poster in front of her. His bright golden eyes, his perfect skin...

"Knock out of it, Blair," she said to herself, shaking her head, trying to shake the strange thoughts from her mind.

She needed to be back home as soon as she could. With a final glance at the poster, Blair turned around and started to make her way back through the city.

Her steps quickened until she was running, her long black boots thumping on the ground. The chilliness and the biting wind were beginning to get to her, making her shiver violently as she ran along the path, heading back to her house.

As Blair reached her small apartment complex, she quickly made it up the stairs to her apartment building's third floor.

Once inside her own apartment, she let out a sigh of relief, leaning her back at her now-closed door.

Her breath coming in ragged gasps, Blair wondered why she felt so restless when she returned.

After a couple of minutes of deep breathing, Blair finally managed to calm herself slightly, and as she was about to pull herself off the door, a knock behind her startled her.

"Blair? Are you in here? It's me..." A voice called from behind the door, sounding muffled. It was Jemima.

"Oh yeah." She sighed, opening the door to let her in.

"Hey, Blair," Jemima said, once she got inside, closing the door behind her, "You look as though you've seen a ghost," Jemima noted, soon as the door was shut behind her. "Not that it's new, but it seems like you saw a bad one," Jemima quickly added, plopping herself on the couch. "By the way, you went for a walk? Your boots are wet, and so is your ridiculous coat," Jemima noted, sizing Blair, who still stood by the door, watching Jemima with an amused look.

Blair nodded. "Yep. I wanted some fresh air," Blair said simply, "And a chance to think, to gather myself, I guess," Blair said, pulling off her coat and hanging it on the rack by the doorway, her boot following next.

"Coffee or chocolate?" Blair asked, padding on the wooden floor with her bare foot towards the kitchen.

"Chocolate, thank you," Jemima replied, picking up one of Blair's books from the table and flicking through it, "so, how did your walk go?" she called out, as Blair rummaged through her cupboard while she awaited the water she had put in the kettle to boil. She grabbed the carton of milk, putting it on the kitchen counter close to the mugs.

"Was okay. A little chilly, and not so much has changed though," Blair responded, turning the now steaming water in both mugs and adding hot cocoa powder and vanilla extract as she stirred them. "How about you? How was your day?" she continued, grabbing the sugar out of the pantry drawer and pouring it into the cups of steaming hot chocolate mix.

"Pretty boring actually," Jemima answered, closing the book and placing it back on the table. "Just like your books," Jemima said with a teasing smile, as Blair came back with a tray of hot chocolate and cookies on it.

"Oh please," Blair said with a smile, handing over Jemima a mug and taking the other herself, before settling on her favorite armchair. "They're quite enjoyable. They're very helpful," Blair stated simply, taking a sip out of her hot chocolate.

Jemima rolled her eyes. "Yeah, sure, whatever makes you sleep well at night, princess." She smirked, and both shared a laugh.

"But then the town, especially the palace, seems busy. Whoever Cadence is, she sure knows how to bring forth an uproar, without even being here!" Jemima complained while taking a sip of her chocolate.

"Mmm," Blair agreed, nodding at Jemima's words. "I wonder too?" Blair then said, setting down her mug on the coffee table, as she leaned against the armchair a bit,

"I'm just curious, you know, whether this Cadence really exists. Or if it's a fake. I mean, if that's even her real name," Jemima commented, looking over at Blair,

"Maybe, maybe not. But whoever she is, she does seem important," Blair said, taking another sip of her chocolate, and watching as the other girl nodded slowly.

"Well, she must have, otherwise, how does she manage to stir such a great disturbance in the whole kingdom of Avronia." Jemima pointed out.

Blair shrugged, "Don't know... Alpha Silas, any idea of where his pack is?" Blair asked, lost in her thoughts.

Jemima tilted her head, "I don't know," she replied, shaking her head, "But he seems terrifying," Jemima said, taking a bite of the cookies Blair had prepared.

"Yeah, I can tell," Blair agreed.

"Why do you suddenly seem interested in this particular case from the palace? You've never indicated interest this much in any other news I bring from the palace?" Jemima raised a brow playfully at her, while she kept munching on her cookies.

Blair shrugged, "I guess I'm curious. I mean, Cadence sounds pretty interesting for an Alpha to be ready to risk his title just to find her," Blair said thoughtfully, smiling slightly.

"Oh, you are intrigued!" Jemima grinned, "That doesn't surprise me at all. You are obsessed, Blair, with everything supernatural you come across," Jemima commented. "So, tell me, did you come across anything interesting today, in your short walk?" she asked, using her fingers to gesture at the last phrase, her dark eyes full of curiosity.

"Nothing much, really." Blair lied, looking down at her now empty mug. "Nothing really seemed out of place though." Blair shrugged. "Just an ordinary day, that is," Blair said with a shrug again.

"Hmm, didn't notice the posters the royal guards were pasting around?" Jemima asked, raising a brow as she took another cookie in her mouth."

"Nope." Blair lied again, seeming disinterested.

"Huh... Well, they were," Jemima pointed out. "I think I grabbed one when no one was looking," she said, dipping her hand in the inner pocket of her coat and pulling out a ruffled and squeezed flier, which she handed to Blair.

Blair took it carefully from her friend's hand, and carefully straightened it. It was the same flier from earlier.

"See?" Jemima said, pointing at it. "It's pretty serious now. The king has declared them wanted criminals cause of the nonexistent witch," Jemima said, giving Blair a knowing grin. "And according to these rumors, she was the most powerful witch in the kingdom about a thousand years ago and aided the werewolves in destroying their arch enemies, the moon stalkers. Afterward, no one ever heard from her again. No trace, nothing," Jemima continued.

Jemima's expression turned into one of curiosity as she watched Blair examine the flier. "What do you make of it?" she questioned, tilting her head.

"Uh... I honestly have no idea what to make of it," Blair admitted, folding the paper back up, as Jemima chuckled softly.

"I mean, obviously, she did something that made the king change sides, since this is all happening right now. But I still can't help but wonder, who she could be?" Jemima explained, shrugging her shoulders, taking another bite of her cookie as Blair sat thinking.

"It's probably just a hoax or a conspiracy story. I'm sorry, I didn't mean to sound skeptical…" Blair trailed off apologetically.

"Whose side you on, sis? Because I'm lost here," Jemima asked, taking the last bite of the cookie.

"We taking sides now?" Blair asked with a chuckle as she got to her feet to take the empty mugs and tray to the kitchen.

"Oh well." Jemima laughed. "I should get going. My break period is over." Jemima got to her feet with a groan as she stretched, "Alright, see you soon!" Blair called from the kitchen, as she heard Jemima make her way to the door.

She heard the front door open and shut.

Blair finished cleaning up in no time and made her way back to her living room.

"She left this," Blair said, picking up the rumpled poster from the couch, slowly taking a seat on the couch, while she studied the poster for the umpteenth time that day.

Blair suddenly felt a wave of drowsiness overwhelm her, as she leaned back on the couch rest, and the poster laid limply on her thigh. She yawned as her eyelids started to feel heavy, then drifted off to sleep.

She dreamt about him…

Chapter Five

"Your little stunt has brought us into fame once more." Lobo, the rogue leader, chuckled dryly, staring at the rumpled poster he held in his hand, which had their pictures on them, declaring them wanted.

"Glad it amuses you," Alpha Silas replied sarcastically, taking a pause from his pacing frenzy and glancing at his companion.

"Let me see it." Otsana, a hybrid from a forbidden union of a werewolf and a witch, and the only female amongst them, who could easily be passed for a male, due to her strong features, her Mohawk haircut and an almost invisible chest region which was always wrapped in a band.

"Jeez. I'm way prettier than what is here in this picture. The artist needs to work on his artistry or something." Otsana stared at the poster with a cringe on her face. "No, man! My nose is way pointer and perfect than this." She kept on with her complaints.

"Take a chill pill OT. It's just a picture," Lubo said with a chuckle, while Alpha Silas rolled his eyes at the display before him.

Otsana sighed dramatically, "They could do better."

"We have more important issues to deal with, and your problem is the fact that your picture isn't as perfect as you are? Women!" Alpha Silas exclaimed suddenly, running his fingers through his hair in a frustrated manner.

"Hey! Yours are much better than mine! Don't diss me like that, Alpha," Otsana retorted angrily, crossing her arms on her chest.

"Are we really doing this now?" Alpha Silas glared at her, his breath labored.

"Oh yeah, here we go," Lubo muttered under his breath as Otsana glared back at the Alpha in front of her.

"Don't you forget so quickly, that you put us in this mess in the first place," Otsana said, not backing down her glare, even with the fact that Alpha Silas' eyes began flickering to gold. Her own gaze turned challenging as her body tensed up in preparation.

"Otsana," Alpha Silas said with gritted teeth, after a short moment of tense silence and a glare competition between them both.

"At this point, it'll be quite hard to differentiate you both from cubs. You're just alike." Lubo shook his head, tired of their daily bants already.

It was over a week already since Alpha Silas, alongside his beta, had approached him to seek help.

He, Lubo, was quite adamant about helping the werewolves of Alpha Silas's clan in searching for the long-lost witch, because, first of all, it was plain crazy.

How do they search for someone who had no authenticity of her existence? Secondly, they were rogues. They never abide by rules. The rogues were mostly made of werewolves who had either been cast away from their clans for rebellion or other intolerable reasons and but a few other supernaturals, including Otsana, the hybridized wolf and witch. She was the only female they had, but could easily be passed as a male due to her taste in clothing and lifestyle too.

Alpha Silas had brought to them a juicy offer. The chance to freely trade and parade on his lands with an agreement of alliance and protection when needed, in exchange for their cooperation in finding the witch before the moon stalkers strike yet again.

The thought of the piercing silver-eyed monsters brought a surge of goosebumps to the skin of Lubo. Though he had never had a close encounter with any of them, their stories were nerve-wracking already.

"Knock it off, you both," Lubo said finally, tired of their endless banters. Alpha Silas and his second in command, Otsana had never gotten along. They fought like lovers, at any chance they both got.

"We have work to do," he said, as he got to his feet and went over to the large table which sat in the middle of the room, where the map was sprawled at.

Alpha Silas gave Otsana one last glare, before moving in two long strides to stand right beside Lubo at the table.

His hands hovered just above it, as his golden eyes scanned every inch of it, looking for some kind of clue, some kind of trace of the witch's location.

"Right here." He started, pointing at a particular spot on the Avronia land map, as Lubo stared intently. "This was where the war happened between the werewolves and the moon stalkers. This was the last place Cadence was found," Alpha Silas said, with a slight shake of the finger, before pointing at another spot. "And there is where the witches resided, with just a magical barrier dividing their land from the wolves,"

"Starting the party without me?" Otsana suddenly cut Alpha Silas short, as she moved one of the chairs by the table in a swift motion and took a seat, crossing her legs.

"Why isn't she out there training alongside the rest again?" Alpha Silas asked Lubo for the umpteenth time, as he couldn't get why his beta wasn't allowed to be in this cave room with him, but Otsana, Lubo's second in command could, and not just that she was only annoying as fuck, she was a challenging female too. She always found new and effective ways of getting right on his nerves.

"Cause she's equally as important as I am here," Lubo said flatly.

Otsana looked over at Alpha Silas, a sly smile playing around her lips. He ignored it.

"We rogues, remember? We do not abide by rules." Otsana reminded Alpha Silas, before turning her attention to Lubo, with an expressionless look on her face.

"Then I want my beta in here," Alpha Silas retorted. "He's equally as useful as she is here."

"As if," Otsana scoffed, as she crossed her arms across her chest. "Lubo and I can take care of whatever is required here. We don't need an extra party. Your presence is suffocating enough," Otsansa spat out.

Alpha Silas' nostrils flared slightly, his canines and claws elongated, and his eyes flickered gold, as he felt Leo at that surface, "Don't test me Otsana," Alpha Silas growled.

"Oh my goddess, I'm so scared, Alpha. Please have mercy," Otsana said dramatically, before rolling her eyes at him.

It took everything in Alpha Silas not to pounce on her that very moment and tear her limb by limb apart, right there and then.

But he controlled himself, seeing it wasn't worth it.

As much as he'd have savored destroying her, he needed her help in finding the witch soon.

"Enough of these childish fighting. I know you hate each other, but we still need to work together," Lubo said with a tired sigh.

"Alpha, your beta, which I'm well aware has been hiding in the shadows all the while, can join us," Lubo said with a shake of his head, as Beta James came out of the shadows and approached where they stood by the table.

"Alpha," James said with a slight bow as he got close. Otsana snickered audibly, while Alpha Silas shot her a dirty glance.

"What were you able to gather on the witch?" Alpha Silas asked his beta, keeping on his cool facade.

Beta James cleared his throat before he spoke. "There's no record of her anywhere. It's almost like she disappeared from the face of the earth," Beta James replied.

"I still don't believe she's gone," Alpha Silas uttered under his breath. "She must have left a trail somewhere. There must be something that would lead us to find her," he said with conviction.

"Otsana," Lubo suddenly called out, his eyes on her.

"No. no." Otsana shook her head, getting to her feet. "I'm not doing that." She shook her head again.

"You're the last resort now," Lubo pleaded. "That's the only way we can find out if she still exists," Lubo reasoned.

"If he really wants to find the witch, then he should find out where she is himself, but I'm not going through that process for him," Otsana declared, shaking her head, her eyes narrowing into slits, as she clenched her jaw.

"There's no other option again Otsana," Lubo sighed. "Just your powers."

"I swear to the goddess," Otsana snarled, clenching and unclenching her fists, "Calm down Otsana," she said to herself, taking in deep breaths, as her eyes fluttered shut. "Unless I get a sincere apology from Alpha Silas, with him admitting he's an ass. I wouldn't do it."

"What are you implying, Otsana?" Alpha Silas growled.

"You know what it means, Alpha Silas," Otsana taunted.

"Why do I even have to apologize to her in the first place?" Alpha Silas asked Lubo calmly.

"Otsana can use her witch powers to find people," Lubo explained.

Alpha Silas was taken aback. "So you're saying, Otsana had the powers to have made this easier for us the whole while, and she made us go round and round in circles trying to find the witch, cause an uproar in the city and gain ourselves criminals of the year? How nice. Just nice." Alpha Silas let out a sarcastic chuckle, moving back a little, shaking his head in amusement.

"You have to understand that it isn't easy for her also. She has a lot to lose too. Using her powers that way has an adverse effect on her too. And seeing you both didn't start on the right foot and are still not moving on the right foot, it might be quite tacky to convince her into using it," Lubo explained.

"I'm standing right here, you know," Otsana said, raising her voice. "Can we please save the drama for later and get this over and done with."

Lubo gave Alpha Silas a look.

"Are you kidding me?" Alpha Silas chuckled in disbelief.

"Please?" Lubo said softly, with a frown. "We're already too invested in this already to do otherwise now."

Alpha Silas rolled his eyes. "Alright," he said, turning over to where Otsana stood. "I'm sorry Otsana," he said.

"I can't hear you," she said, watching Alpha Silas's face contour in a frown and his teeth gritted. She enjoyed every bit of his struggle.

"Otsana. I know we both started on the wrong foot. Can we please drop our differences and start up again on a fresh template? I'm sorry for being an ass earlier," Alpha Silas pleaded.

Otsana let out a sigh, sensing the sincerity in his voice.

"Alright, I'll do it," she said finally, with a shrug. "As long as it gets us our answers fast," she said, looking at Lubo, who nodded in agreement.

"Thank you," Alpha Silas said gratefully, with a small relieved grin.

"Doesn't still make us friends, though," Otsana said, as she walked to the middle of the room and began drawing a circle with white chalk on the floor, getting into the middle of the circle, sitting with crossed legs in it, before starting the chant.

Everyone watched as Otsana raised her hands above her head and closed her eyes whilst muttering words in a language none of them recognized.

After a few minutes, Otsana opened her eyes, still chanting.

A bright light radiated from her body, enveloping everyone inside the room in a dazzling glow, as Otsana's eyes suddenly turned all white, and her head jerked upwards in a quick motion as a loud crack echoed across the room, and the lights blinking rapidly, all at once, till it came to an abrupt stop.

A deafening silence fell upon the room as everyone's eyes widened, and they stared at each other, waiting for some kind of explanation, but none appeared.

Until Otsana finally spoke up. Her head still held up, and her eyes upturned.

"Cadence is alive and lives right at the main city of Avronia," she said slowly.

"Where exactly?" Alpha Silas asked as he moved closer.

"The main city of Avronia," Otsana repeated slowly.

"How do I locate her?" Alpha Silas questioned, but instead of a response, Otsana began jerking.

"OT!" Lubo exclaimed, rushing to her side.

Her body jerked violently as it arched forward and back, until finally falling backward onto the ground with a thud.

She lay unmoving, her eyes closed.

Chapter Six

Blair woke up with a terrible headache yet again.

It's been three days in a row, and she kept having dreams of the yellow-eyed werewolf. He always looked for her, and this time, he found her.

She sat up on her bed, wondering why it felt really chilly all of a sudden.

"I thought I shut the windows?" she said to herself as she looked over to her window, which was now slightly agape.

"Strange," she muttered, getting to her feet from her bed, as she picked up her night robe and draped it around her shoulders, walking up to her window.

The chilly breeze waved past her face as she stood by the window, staring at the starry sky. It all felt like deja vu.

The moon was full, the stars twinkled down on her, and the gentle breeze caressed her skin as it flowed through her hair.

Her body started to tingle, she couldn't explain exactly how, but something was wrong.

Flashes of the dreams she had been getting for the past few days came to mind. The feeling that she was missing something was there too.

Something felt off. But what was she missing? Her head pounded harder as her brow creased.

"Stop thinking about it," she told herself as she closed her eyes tightly, letting out a frustrated sigh, "You are just being paranoid again." Blair opened her eyes, took a deep breath, and then turned around, shutting her window close and walked back into her room. She plopped down in her bed once more, trying to ignore the niggling feeling she could feel growing inside her stomach. The night was still young and hopefully, sleep would certainly be able to help alleviate the sensation.

As Blair lay in her bed, tossing and turning until dawn broke, she wondered if the werewolf was somehow connected to the visions.

***

Blair woke up as if in a daze. Her senses seemed sluggish. Even her mind felt slow. It was almost like her mind was detached from her body.

Like everything around her had stopped working for a minute or two.

She blinked slowly as she lifted her arm from across her forehead to look at the grandpa's wall clock, which hung overhead. 10:15 A.M... Great. It was past her coffee time.

She groaned softly as she tried to force herself out of bed and to the bathroom.

Blair yawned as she stepped into her tiny bathroom.

She glanced at the mirror and grimaced when she saw that her reflection didn't have any energy left in it.

She stared at her tired blue eyes and rubbed them before splashing some water onto her face and brushing her teeth.

Then she put her toothbrush away and brushed her messy, tangled brown hair that she kept in a loose ponytail.

"Eissh." Blair winced as the icy cold water from the taps touched her skin, as she stepped in to shower.

"E wela," Blair whispered, as she watched the icy cold water steam up before stepping back in.

The warm water felt great against her sore muscles, easing her sore body and calming her mind.

Her mind went blank as she let the hot water soothe the knots and tension that formed in her muscles. Blair stood under the spray for a few minutes, letting the steam clear her mind. After several more moments, Blair stepped out of the shower and dried herself off.

She walked out of the bathroom, her towel wrapped around her body and her wet hair and walked back into her room.

She grabbed a long flowing gown out of her closet and slipped into it. The fabric felt soft and comforting, and she immediately felt better, as she began combing her long, flowing hair.

Once dressed, Blair exited the room and headed toward the kitchen to make breakfast for herself. It was her favorite morning ritual, and she enjoyed making breakfast for herself.

"No, no, no," Blair muttered, as she opened her cupboard to see she was running low on groceries, and there wasn't even enough to fix herself breakfast.

"This isn't happening," Blair said with a sigh, as she refused to acknowledge the hard fact that she had to go to the market soon enough.

She grabbed her basket and covered her hair and face with a scarf, before making her way out of her apartment to the market.

Blair walked through the streets, heading towards the market. She could hear the familiar chirping sounds of birds from where they flew above her.

Everything seemed normal and peaceful. No one seemed to pay much attention to the woman who was wandering the streets alone, wearing an oversized flowing gown and a scarf over her head, carrying a large market bag on her shoulder.

Except for the small part of her that seemed to be hyper aware of everything around her.

After half an hour, Blair finally reached the marketplace.

The sun beat down on the market, warming her skin and warming her heart, giving her goosebumps from the coolness outside. She loved shopping here whenever she got to step out, with the bright colors, fresh produce, and wonderful aromas wafting around her.

Blair made her way over to the fruit section, looking at fruits and vegetables while taking occasional bites from her freshly baked scone she bought from a vendor not so long ago. She sighed happily, closing her eyes and enjoying the pleasant atmosphere. Blair finished her scone before she heard a rustle behind her.

Blair quickly turned around. Her heart began to pound faster as she saw a couple of royal guards marching in her direction.

She took an unconscious step back and pulled on the scarf to further conceal her face.

The guards walked past her without a second glance, ignoring her entirely.

Blair let out a sigh of relief. She was just being paranoid.

She knew no one knew, and she was safe. But still, she couldn't get rid of the tingling sensation, which made her feel something big and unavoidable was going to happen soon.

***

Blair returned to her apartment a little later than usual that day after she had managed to avoid the guards.

She walked into the building, her bag held close to her chest. She felt uneasy as she walked up the stairs to her floor. She could sense something was off, and she hated the sensation.

Finally reaching her door, Blair unlocked it with the spare key that she had tucked in her purse.

But before she could step in, she heard a loud commotion in the building. The royal guards were in the building, and so were the wanted rogues too.

Blair felt the anxiety start to rise as she hurriedly ran into the safety of her apartment, slamming the door shut and locking it again.

The sound of heavy thumping was coming from the hallway leading to her floor, and she froze as her body tensed up.

What were these guys doing here?

Blair took a peep out her window to see what was happening outside, and sure enough, she saw the royal guards parading around in search of the criminals that were on the run.

After a while, the noise died down, and the royal guards made their way to another floor.

Blair let out a sigh of relief, and she slumped against her door with relief flooding her body.

"Please open up!" A voice suddenly called out from across her apartment with a loud bang, startling her, as she jumped to her feet.

"Go away!" She heard one of her neighbors scream out and shut their door on them.

"Open up, please!" They called out, pounding on the next door.

It sounded like they were trying to break down the door.

Blair quickly opened her door and peeped out to see two men and a lady, who didn't seem like a lady, just like in the poster, trying to find a place to hide.

"Psst. Come on in," she silently called out and gestured to them as she opened her door wider to let them in.

They all rushed in, as Blair looked across the hallway to ensure that no one saw them enter her apartment before she shut the door, locking it.

They looked exhausted, disheveled, dirty and sweaty, but relieved all the same.

"Thank you so much," The one who she recognized as the Alpha said to her, as he bowed his head deeply as he smiled at her, before he straightened his posture.

The one who graced her dreams for the past three nights now.

Suddenly it was beginning to make a little more sense to her.

They were destined to meet. But her concern was on the fact that werewolves and her kind were in a feud, all thanks to the war which happened a thousand years ago.

He looked to be in his mid-twenties. He looked more handsome and dangerous in a hot and sexy way in person.

His black curly hair was slicked back and clean. His golden eyes were wide and alert. His pale cheeks had some dark shadows beneath his eyes, but overall he looked very healthy.

Blair found him rather attractive and couldn't help herself from staring at his perfectly sculpted features.

She felt uncomfortable under his intense stare, but tried her best to play it cool by crossing her arms over her chest and looking unbothered.

The other man, who looked rougher than any of them, said to her, as he gave her a nod of acknowledgment.

Blair nodded back, unsure of what else to say or do.

"Yeah, thank you," The only female amongst them said as she made herself comfortable, settling down on one of the chairs.

"Excuse our manners," the Alpha spoke up, giving a glare to the lady who rolled her eyes in response, as he walked closer to Blair, stretching his hand towards her for a handshake.

"My name is Alpha Silas, and these are my companions, Lubo and Otsana." Blair took his stretched hand and blinked at the sudden surge of electricity that moved through her skin, once her hand came in contact with his.

Blair blushed as she shook his hand quickly and dropped his hand before taking a step back.

"Blair," She breathed, trying to calm the erratic beating of her heart and ease the tingling feeling that was growing inside her.

The Alpha's eyes narrowed at her response, but he didn't speak. He simply watched Blair carefully as she continued to eye Lubo and Otsana with apprehension.

Otsana gave Blair a small smile and waved. Blair offered a nervous smile and waved back, trying her best not to look intimidated by Otsana.

"We are very sorry for the intrusion, and we really appreciate your kind gesture to hide us here," Alpha Silas said calmly to Blair.

Lubo added, "Thank you so much for allowing us to stay here."

"I'm glad. Do make yourself comfortable," Blair said softly as she gestured to the couch and chairs in front of her fireplace.

Both men glanced around and then settled themselves in the cushions of her couch, immediately pulling out a map and some of their tools, and dropping them on the coffee table before them.

Blair glanced at them, surprised that they had brought those things with them, but before she could react, they heard loud stomps on her floor again. The royal guards were back.

"Fuck," Alpha Silas muttered out, as they all got to their feet alert.

"Open up in the name of the King!" One of the royal guards cried out. "We have been authorized to search for the wanted criminals!"

"Quick," Blair whispered to her visitors, leading them to her basement to hide them while they waited out the storm.

The trio climbed into the tight space, as Blair locked the door to the basement with the key. When she was done, she walked back to her living room. The guards were almost at her door now.

"Open up, or we'll be forced to break down your door!" Came the loud voice of a royal guard as he pounded on her door.

"Coming," Blair said as she got to the door.

Letting out a deep sigh and being positive about the fact that she had successfully masked their scent, she pulled the door open. The royal guards were already surrounding her home, and Blair could feel their stares drilling holes into her. She stared back as hard as she could at the tall, dark-haired, dark-eyed male standing right before her.

"Where are they?"

Chapter Seven

"Ouch. You're stepping on me," Otsana mumbled angrily, as she felt one of the men's shoes on her leg.

"Sorry. It's too tight in here," Lubo apologized, trying to shift away from Otsana in the tight basement space they found themselves in.

He could barely move a muscle as he was stuck in the cramped position.

The floor had no visible surface for him to rest and sit on. There were only wood walls and ceiling around them.

There wasn't even any ventilation to be felt with how small it seemed.

It was almost pitch black.

All they could see was the silhouette of each other, with the little light that seeped in through the cracks between the wood cracks enough to barely illuminate their bodies, but not much more than that.

"Damn, you reek Lubo." Otsana cringed her nose in disgust, as a pungent odor emanated from the armpit of his shirt. She couldn't imagine what kind of bodily waste he collected in the form of sweat. The smell alone made her gag. "You need a shower."

"Not my fault we've been on the run for the past few days now," he replied defensively, rubbing his neck, "At least I got fresh clothes this time, though." Lubo looked at his worn-out outfit from last night. "I can't believe they've just been chasing us so long with no luck in finding the witch." He let out an irritated sigh.

"Finding the witch isn't the problem right now. The only problem we have now is the fact that I'm close to passing out from the smell oozing out from you," Otsana said, her voice raised a bit.

"Can you both knock it off already?" Alpha Silas, who had been quiet for the whole ordeal, spoke calmly. His eyes were closed. He leaned against the wall, looking very relaxed, like he had no worries about the world.

Lubo scowled while Otsana rolled her eyes. "What is with everyone today? First, our efforts to find the witch is futile. Secondly, we get chased by the guards all around the city, and now we are hiding in a basement that isn't fit for a person. Talk more of three grown-ass wolves, having us breathe in toxic air," she said exasperatedly.

Alpha Silas opened his eyes, glaring at her briefly.

She could tell that the moment was going to come when he'd snap back at her because Otsana knew how to push his buttons like none other.

But then he just sighed heavily instead.

"Look, Otsana. We're all tired and in this mess together. Cut some slack and stop acting as though you're in this alone," Alpha Silas said with a calm tone.

His statement brought silence in the basement.

The tension slowly ebbed, the group falling into a somewhat amicable silence once again.

They heard a noise up above, of a key turning in the lock.

The basement door swung open, letting sunlight and air stream into the room.

"They are gone," Blair said with a smile as she opened the door wider to let them out.

Otsana was the first to step out immediately, as she stretched her neck and body and took in a lungful of clean air for what felt like the first time in hours.

Lubo and Alpha Silas followed next, moving out to the living space.

"You all must be tired," Blair said, leading them back to the living room. "I've prepared baths for you all. Only you have to take turns, obviously," Blair added, smiling at her joke. "While I'll fix dinner."

"That would be nice. Thank you, Blair," Alpha Silas answered warmly.

"Sure, Alpha." She smiled.

"I'll go first!" Otsana announced eagerly, as she began searching for the bathroom herself. "Where's the bathroom at?" she called out.

"Second door down the hall. There are towels in there already," Blair called back.

Otsana thanked her before disappearing into the bathroom, taking one of the spare towels with her.

The water warmed up quickly after Otsana had stepped into the tub. She let out a deep sigh of contentment once she felt herself visibly relax.

"I have another bathroom, though, if you're in a hurry to wash up too," Blair said to Alpha Silas, who seemed a little uncomfortable. "Only that it hasn't been used for a while now, and it's a little cramped up," she quickly added.

"It's fine, I'll manage." Alpha Silas assured with a nod, as Blair led him to a smaller bathroom which was a door close to the kitchen.

"There you go." She pointed to the door.

"Thank you," Alpha Silas said, getting into the bathroom.

"Aren't you done already?" Blair heard Lubo's voice down the hallway, right at the bathroom door Otsana was. "I need to use the bathroom too," he whined.

"You wait for your turn." Blair heard Otsana say.

She let out a chuckle, shaking her head as she walked to the kitchen to get something done.

Good thing she had done her grocery shopping earlier, so there was enough to make a feast for her unexpected visitors.

As she started slicing various vegetables, making a salad, she was so engrossed in what she did, that she didn't notice when a shirtless Alpha Silas, with droplets of water dripping on his torso, made his way into the kitchen.

"I couldn't find the towels," Alpha Silas said, startling Blair, as she turned over to him.

Her mouth went dry, seeing the Alpha's hot body right before her.

She swallowed thickly before speaking, "The... the towels are on the rack, close to the door. I'll help you grab some," she mumbled hastily, still unable to look away from his muscled body.

His hands landed softly on her arm, sending waves of tingles throughout her body.

"Don't worry about it. I dry up real quick." Alpha Silas stared at her with a smile.

"Oh, okay, if you say so." Blair cleared her throat, gently pulling her hand from his soft grasp.

"So... What can I assist with?" Alpha Silas asked, looking around the kitchen curiously, his eyes landing on the chopping board.

Blair shrugged, putting aside the knife, picking up the bowl full of lettuce and tomato. "Can you chop them?" she asked, staring up at him questioningly.

"Yeah sure." Alpha Silas nodded, grabbing the bowl from her.

"You don't need to grab that," Blair said with a chuckle, retrieving the bowl of veggies and placing them on the kitchen counter.

"This is what you need." She placed the chopping board with a cutting knife before him. "There you go."

As soon as he grabbed a handful of lettuce and started cutting into it, Blair tried her best to hide a giggle at how clumsy Alpha Silas appeared to be.

Even with how strong he looked when he was working. The way his brow furrowed slightly, as he concentrated, as he kept missing some pieces of lettuce or tomatoes.

"Are you sure you've been in a kitchen your whole life? Cause you look like you're going through a lot right now," Blair said, as she noticed the sweat stains on his skin and clothes. It was really starting to bother her.

He gave her a lopsided grin. "No, I haven't been to the kitchen. I mean, what's a kitchen?" Alpha Silas asked, with a huge smile playing on his lips, while he kept murdering the veggies.

"Oh yeah, I see what you did there." Blair laughed, shaking her head lightly.

"What did I do?" he asked with a smirk.

"You killed the vegetables. Now they're horrible looking." Blair laughed.

"What?! No, they're not! They're beautiful!" He argued, placing his hand over his chest, as though he got hurt.

"No, they're hideous," she said firmly.

"You're just jealous 'cause you can't cut lettuce, as beautiful as I do." He teased, smirking slightly.

"Oh please." Blair laughed. Retrieving the knife from him and taking his spot, she began rechopping the veggies.

Alpha Silas watched her, admiring her slender yet muscular fingers dancing gracefully across the counter. Her movements were graceful.

Like how his were.

He could feel the urge to reach out and hold her hand, touch her, feel her smooth skin under his fingertips.

Just as he thought about doing so, however, Blair moved her attention over to him, giving him that playful yet challenging look she always gave him.

He held her gaze for a second longer. An awkward silence stretched between them both as their eyes locked.

Alpha Silas found himself lost in her chocolate brown eyes, as she returned the same expression.

Both of them felt a slight heat rise onto their faces.

A loud cough suddenly broke the silence, and Blair snapped her eyes away from his, quickly looking at her hands and blushing furiously.

Alpha Silas cleared his throat awkwardly as he scratched the back of his head, averting his gaze from Lubo and Otsana, who had just joined them in the kitchen.

"Seems like I interrupted something." Otsana hummed as she picked up an apple from the grocery bag and began munching on it, while she raised herself up to sit on the counter, dangling her leg from it.

"Not exactly," Alpha Silas replied, trying to compose himself as he avoided looking at either Blair or Otsana.

"We were just making dinner," Alpha Silas defended.

"Must be one hell of a staring meal," Lubo snorted, rolling his eyes as he leaned against the wall. "I'm so famished, I could eat a cow right now." He yawned.

Blair chuckled, shaking her head as she set the other ingredients she would need to prepare a large-course dinner.

She had decided on the turkey. As well as some side dishes, and mashed potatoes, with lots of gravy.

"What can I help with?" Otsana asked, jumping back down to her feet to assist Blair.

"The last time I got free help, I ended up paying for it." Blair joked, as her eyes trailed to Alpha Silas.

"I wasn't that bad!" Alpha Silas defended with widened eyes, making Blair giggle.

"Oh please. I'm better in the kitchen than that entitled jughead," Otsana said, grabbing on the raw turkey Blair brought by to dress it.

"Otsana." Alpha Silas warned with gritted teeth.

Otsana scoffed, throwing a glare at him. "Deal with it." Otsana huffed, turning her attention towards Blair. "Did you cook the potatoes too?" Otsana asked as Blair grabbed the potato masher.

"Yeah," Blair said.

Otsana smiled happily. "My favorite! Let me help with that too, once I'm done with this."

"You're already helping out on a lot already, don't worry about it." Blair smiled.

"Nope, we literally owe you our lives for saving us. It's only fair I help with this," Otsana reasoned.

"Well, if it's not any trouble," Blair replied, smiling gratefully, grateful for Otsana's help.

"Of course, it isn't any trouble. Don't be silly. Now come on, help me finish," Otsana said, pushing the masher and the potatoes toward Blair.

"Uhm, it's obvious we aren't needed here again," Lubo noted, as he pushed himself off the wall. "What do you do for fun over here?" Lubo asked, leaving the kitchen, with Alpha Silas trailing behind.

"I have loads of books!" Blair called back.

"Boring!" Lubo snorted.

Blair smiled and kept on with what she was doing with the help of Otsana in preparing the mashed potatoes.

After the two finished everything they needed to do, Blair and Otsana took the turkey off the oven and placed it on its wooden platter, along with the other vegetables.

They took care of the salad and prepared the rest of the ingredients as well as the stuffing and sauce for the turkey.

When they were finished cooking, they both set the dining table together, and they all settled to eat.

"Finally." Lubo groaned in satisfaction, as he grabbed a cutlery to dig in.

"Pig." Otsana rolled her eyes, as she dug in too.

"This is so good," Alpha Silas moaned as he took a bite.

Blair smiled at their reactions.

"So Blair," Lubo started, still munching on his food, and gaining her attention.

"What supernatural are you? Because I don't smell any wolf."

Blair paled, as she felt the blood drain off her face.

Chapter Eight

"You're not a werewolf, right? Or are you? Your wolf is concealed?" Lubo asked all at once, still munching on his food loudly, oblivious to the tension that was building up on the table.

"I... Er," Blair stuttered.

"Let her be already Lubo!" Otsana intervened, noticing the discomfort on Blair's face.

"Don't mind him, Blair. He's just as insensitive as his third member," Otsana spat, glaring daggers at Lubo.

"What did I do now?" Lubo asked, looking confused, as he stared back at Otsana.

"Dickhead," Otsana said, returning her attention back to her food and totally ignoring Lubo, who shrugged and took his attention back to his food.

Alpha Silas, who had been silent during the whole ordeal, couldn't help but watch Blair with keen interest. He really didn't know what was about her, but he seemed intrigued by her. Her demeanor, her hospitality, her elegance, even though she seemed shy, her beauty, her smile... her smile, he recalled it from back in the kitchen. For some reason, it made him feel things he never thought he had in him to feel.

Her scent... Alpha Silas found himself feeling overwhelmed by her scents. True, she didn't smell like she had a wolf hidden within her, but she gave off that same unique scent that he couldn't place what she was.

He could sense a surge of power from her, but he still was confused about what exactly she was.

"Beta James," he called through his mind link.

"Alpha." The beta was back at the pack's territory, overseeing the business of the clan while he, the Alpha, was on the run.

"What's the update?" Alpha Silas asked. "Is the pack doing alright? Any new attacks?"

"No Alpha, there have been no new attacks, and everything has been going fine. We've added more guards at the borders, and we're currently on the lookout for whoever or whatever creatures are behind this," Beta James informed the alpha. "But asides from that, everything is all good."

"Good, good, thank you. Keep me updated," Alpha Silas replied.

"Yes, Alpha," Beta James acknowledged.

"Beta James." The Alpha called through his mind link again, his eyes on Blair, while she kept munching on her food.

"Alpha."

"I need you to run a tab on someone for me," Alpha Silas requested.

"Okay Alpha?" Beta awaited further instruction.

"Her name is Blair. I have a strong feeling she isn't a she-wolf, but I can't place what exactly she is, I need more information on her. She actually saved me and the gang, housing us too," Alpha Silas said. "So run an evaluation and if you find anything out, call me immediately."

"Of course, Alpha, I'll get started immediately," Beta James said.

"Thank you." Alpha Silas agreed before ending the mind link.

He turned his attention back to the woman, sitting across him at the dining table, eating silently with an air around her that told Alpha Silas that he would not be able to decipher what she was thinking or feeling.

He decided to take action and spoke without much preamble.

"So tell me, what do you do Blair?" he asked, genuinely curious.

Blair almost choked on her food when she heard him. "What do you mean?" she asked, using a napkin to wipe her mouth and swallowing hard.

"Nothing really," she answered, looking down at her intertwined fingers on her lap. "I just help people where I can."

"Oh, I see," Alpha Silas said, nodding his head, not intending to pry further.

Silence fell upon the table once more. Everyone was lost in their thoughts as they finished up their dinner.

Blair grabbed the now empty dishes, politely declining the offer of Otsana to help, as she began picking up the empty dishes from the table.

"Nope. I'll take mine." Alpha Silas stopped her from taking his. "And Lubo's too," he said, getting to his feet and grabbing Lubo's plate alongside his.

"Thanks," Blair said gratefully. "But you didn't have to," Blair said as she made her way to the kitchen to do the dishes, with Alpha Silas right at her trail.

"It wasn't a problem. It was my pleasure." Alpha Silas assured her, making sure she was okay with him doing the barest minimum.

Once they reached the kitchen, they both dropped the plates into the sink.

Blair moved back towards the countertop and began filling the sink with soapy water to wash off the dirty dishes.

"What can I help with?" Alpha Silas asked, looking at her expectantly.

"Grab the dry towel from the rack, you'll wipe off the water from the dishes, once I'm done," she said, pointing towards where the towel hung.

"Oh, okay," Alpha Silas said, grabbing the towel from the rack, and began wiping off the dishes she was done with, while she continued cleaning the dirty ones in the sink. "Hey," Blair called to Alpha Silas, who was so dedicated to his work.

"Yeah... What-" Alpha Silas stopped mid-sentence as Blair rubbed part of the suds on his nose, giggling out immediately.

"What was that for?!" Alpha Silas demanded, wiping his nose with the back of his sleeve with a smile playing on his lips.

Blair chuckled lightly, "Your nose looked funny when it got wet!" She said.

The corner of Alpha Silas's mouth pulled upwards into a grin, "Well, I guess I'll get to know how funny it looks on you," he said, dipping his hand in the soapy water.

"Hold on. No, no, no." Blair shifted back, laughing as Alpha Silas rubbed it on her nose and part of her face.

"That's not fair!" Blair laughed out, playfully pushing him away from her.

"I don't play fair baby," Alpha Silas said as they both kept playing with the suds.

They continued this for several minutes until suddenly Blair's head snapped towards the clock.

"Damn. What have we done?" she said, staring around the kitchen which was now filled with soapy foams all around them.

"Shit, sorry!" Alpha Silas said, then they both shared a laugh.

"Come on, let me clean up, and then we can go back to meet the others before they wonder why the dishes are taking so long to do," Blair said after the laughter died down.

"Sure." Alpha Silas followed her lead, helping her put everything in place.

They returned to the dining room and found Otsana and Lubo seated with serious faces, as they had the map sprawled before them.

"Took you long enough," Otsana said, not looking up.

Blair noticed the sudden change of tides in the atmosphere. She wondered what might have transpired while they were back in the kitchen.

"What's wrong guys?" Alpha Silas asked, pulling a seat and settling in it.

Lubo gestured at him, and he got the hint immediately.

"Uhm, Blair, could you please give us a moment, please?" Alpha Silas asked, giving Blair an apologetic look.

"Yes, sure." Blair nodded, walking over to her room, understanding fully well that they needed privacy.

After closing the door to the bedroom behind her, Blair leaned against it, closing her eyes for a brief second, trying to collect her emotions, and failing miserably because every emotion she felt was conflicting, all mixed together.

There was confusion, fear, and curiosity. And the most powerful one was longing.

She opened her eyes, and turned towards the large window in front of her, looking out on the moonlit night, the stars twinkling brilliantly in the darkness.

"What is the trouble?" Alpha Silas asked as Blair was out of earshot.

"We should be asking you that, Alpha," Otsana retorted, sounding extremely pissed. "You seem to have forgotten the reason why we are out here. Instead of us looking for a way to find the witch, that's if there's a witch. But no. You're here flirting with the one who has been nothing but helpful to us," Otsana said harshly, her voice full of anger.

"Otsana, that's not... We're not... We weren't..." Alpha Silas tried to protest.

"Save it," Otsana interrupted him. "You placed us in this mess. We've gotten more royal troops on our tail than ever since we began our rogue race. So excuse me, Alpha, if we're a little skeptical about your intentions," Otsana spat out the last word like it had been sour on her tongue.

"Otsana," Lubo said in a calm tone, urging her to chill out a bit.

"No Lubo," Otsana protested. "He brought us in on this, and he gets to do what he wants too! That's not how it is meant to go," Otsana argued stubbornly.

"Enough!" Alpha Silas growled out, causing the table to ramble at its effect, his eyes flickering gold, as he huffed angrily, he could feel his wolf, struggling to surface. The wolf inside of him roared in frustration at what Omega was saying. "How dare you! How dare you accuse me of doing anything other than acting in a good and honorable way! Do not speak to me with such disrespect!" He snarled out furiously.

"Then act with the same decency!" Otsana shot back, equally angered by his words.

"Or what?" Alpha Silas challenged, daring the woman to respond.

"Or else we will make you regret ever coming into our home, to seek for us and ask for our help!" Otsana threatened, looking at Alpha Silas with venom in her eyes.

"And what makes you think I need you" Alpha Silas screamed out.

"Why would I need any assistance from you or anyone else? I've been doing fine on my own."

"Maybe you are, maybe you're not," Otsana spat, rising to her feet in her anger. "And maybe we shouldn't have bothered listening to your bullshit when you came to us seeking help!" She threw Alpha Silas's words in his face.

Alpha Silas stood up to match her height, "What did you just say?" He growled out menacingly.

"Are you deaf? I said you didn't deserve any help," Otsana yelled back. "You didn't come here asking for our help. You came here to use us for your own gain! Because we were here, and you thought we had what you wanted!"

"Don't be ridiculous," Alpha Silas scoffed.

"Why would I want to use you? Why the hell would I ever want anyone, let alone the likes of you, to assist me?"

"You don't get to make those kinds of assumptions," Alpha Silas replied, still glaring daggers at the female.

"You know what, fuck this! Fuck you and this stupid mission. Lubo and I will take our leave now." Otsana turned over and met eyes with Lubo, who rose to his feet beside Otsana.

"Lubo?" Alpha Silas looked with surprise at Lubo, who had been quiet through the whole fight. "You're leaving too?" he questioned, sounding shocked.

"I'm sorry Alpha, but I need to leave too," Lubo explained, placing a hand on Alpha Silas's shoulder. "Things don't always turn out the way they seem. I hope you find what you're looking for," Lubo said with an apologetic look.

Alpha Silas watched, stunned, as both Otsana and Lubo walked out of the house, shutting the door behind them.

For a few seconds, Alpha Silas stared at the closed door, lost for words and feeling completely bewildered about the entire situation.

He shook himself out of his daze and fell back on the chair, bowing his head and using both his hands to hold his head tightly. He took deep breaths and focused on calming the raging fire inside of him, and the raging fury he felt.

When he eventually raised his head back up, he sighed deeply and stood up, looking at the maps strewn across the table.

He gathered the papers and replaced them back in the pack where they had it hidden.

Then walked over to the fireplace and knelt in front of it, putting a single log on the fire. Once the fire had begun to blaze brightly again, he took a seat right before the fireplace, watching it burn, as his thoughts swirled everywhere, all at once.

Chapter Nine

Blair woke up with a throbbing headache. Her entire body felt heavy, as though a full bucket of stones had been thrown on her body while she slept.

She groaned as she opened her eyes, the room was too bright, and it took her a few seconds to adjust.

The sun shone right into her open eyelids, causing a huge impact on her migraine.

She rubbed her forehead slowly and then moved to sit up, her muscles feeling sore and weak as she did so.

She winced as she raised herself from her bed.

She knew using her powers was going to have an adverse effect, but she never imagined it was going to be this extreme. Her body was on fire.

It felt like a million tiny needles were stabbing at her brain all at once.

Blair sighed deeply. This wasn't something new.

The problem was her headaches had been growing worse lately, and now that was something to be bothered about.

She knew that exerting that much power she did the day before to conceal their scent from the royal guards and concealed hers too from them, was going to cost a lot, but she never imagined it to be this extreme.

It had been years since she'd last experienced this kind of pain.

She closed her eyes and let out a deep sigh, trying hard not to let the pain overwhelm her right away as the burning sensation in her head intensified.

She sat there for another few minutes, just waiting patiently until she finally felt some sort of relief, although the headache didn't seem to get any better.

Blair opened her eyes and sat up. As her vision came back into focus, it came to her notice that the house was as quiet as it had always been the day before.

She knew she had blacked out almost immediately when she got back into her room. But she could remember hearing their voices raised to some point, as though they were having an argument of some sort.

She wasn't awake long enough to know.

Blair stood up and stretched slowly and carefully to alleviate some of the tension in her body, as she walked to her room door. She paused as she was still halfway through her stretching and listened attentively.

The silence was palpable.

She made her presence known in the living room, expecting to see the werewolves either sleeping or up and doing.

She suddenly felt bad about the fact that she hadn't provided them with the sleeping necessities before she had crashed the night before.

At least she'd have invited Otsana to sleep in her room with her, since she was the only female amongst her gang.

Speaking of which, Blair recalled she had perceived another scent aside from her wolf on Otsana, but it was too swift for her to decide. Or she might have possibly just imagined it.

Either way, Blair couldn't help feeling guilty for sleeping through all this.

She looked around the living space to see just Alpha Silas lying in an awkward position, fast asleep.

His snores filled the air, making him look even more like a sleepy lion cub. A smile curled up one side of her face involuntarily at his cute antics.

Even though he acted all gruff and scary most times, he also was quite sweet inside. She wondered what else he was hiding underneath the surface. He certainly seemed to be a very complicated person.

She sighed, walking to the kitchen to check if Otsana or Lubo was there, as she saw no sign of them anywhere.

"Otsana?" she called out softly, walking toward the basement to search for her. She heard no reply. "Lubo?" Still no answer.

She walked back to the living room to see Alpha Silas awake and seated, lost in space.

"Alpha Silas. You're awake, good morning," Blair said, moving closer.

"They left," Alpha Silas said without looking up.

"They left? I don't understand," Blair said as she stood close to the alpha.

"Otsana and Lubo quit on me and left." Alpha Silas looked up at Blair, his face blank and devoid of anything other than anger.

Blair frowned, puzzled by Alpha Silas's words. "Why? What happened?" Blair asked bewildered, taking a seat beside him.

"No need to be modest about it. I know you heard it all last night." Alpha Silas scoffed.

"Heard what exactly? I didn't hear anything. I slept off almost immediately," Blair explained.

Alpha Silas narrowed his eyes slightly. "Oh. Well, that's fine, I guess." He shrugged nonchalantly.

"What happened?" Blair asked again, confused.

He leaned back on his chair and closed his eyes. "Maybe they are right, and this search is futile. And indeed, she doesn't exist."

"Okay..." Blair said slowly, unsure what else she should say in response to that strange comment, but urging him to carry on.

The atmosphere became tense as they both fell into an awkward silence. It was Blair who broke the silence first, "So, what does all this mean?"

"We have no leads here. We've checked everywhere we can think of and still haven't found anything about her anywhere. So, that leaves us with nothing and the conclusion that Cadence was just a fairytale or indeed she disappeared from the face of the earth." Alpha Silas sighed. His mood grew gloomy. "This is the end. My whole efforts will come to nothing."

"No." Blair shook her head vehemently. "I mean you've come this far already. Will you just give up this easily?"

"What else is there to do? This is literally the end of the road for me," Alpha Silas said bitterly.

Blair hesitated for a moment. Then she said, "What if I can find a way?" she said,

"How?" Alpha Silas asked, his interest piqued.

"Soon," Blair said with a smile playing on her lips.

Alpha Silas raised an eyebrow at her, asking, "Are you sure?"

"Definitely." Blair nodded. "I promise."

"How do you plan on doing that? How could you possibly make the impossible possible?" Alpha Silas asked skeptically.

"Don't underestimate my abilities, Alpha Silas," Blair smirked.

"Let's get prepared," she said, getting to her feet.

"Prepared for?" He raised a brow at her.

"I want to take you somewhere," Blair called back, as she made her way to the bathroom to freshen up.

***

"I still don't get why you insisted on us walking," Alpha Silas complained for the umpteenth time, as they kept walking further down.

"And you're supposed to be the strong one here." Blair laughed out, as she kept leading them down the street.

"This stuff is really hot and itchy," He complained, tugging on the coat he had over him to disguise him since he was still on the run.

"You'll be fine." Blair chuckled.

The street was quiet at this time of the day, most people either working or shopping.

The sun was shining brightly in the sky, and birds were chirping happily.

It made Blair's stomach rumble as they continued to walk along the street. They passed several cafes and stores and soon reached a large park.

A little path led into the park itself. It was a small pathway that connected the two sides of the park. At the entrance was a big bronze gate.

They both made their way in and entered the park.

It appeared to be completely deserted, but still beautiful.

"Come on," Blair said, leading them both through a path in the park that led further into the woods.

"Are you sure you know where we are headed?" Alpha Silas asked, looking around the unfamiliar surroundings.

"Scared much?" Blair teased, walking straight ahead.

Not long after, the sound of a waterfall was heard.

"We are here already!" She squealed happily, following its source until they arrived, where they heard the waterfall.

The view was magnificent, huge, with tons of flowers blooming, but also surrounded by trees.

"Well..." Blair smiled at the sight. "Here we are."

"Where is this?" he questioned, staring at the scenery.

"My safe space," Blair said with a smile, closing her eyes and taking in the scenery.

Silas followed suit shortly after.

The scenery was absolutely breathtaking. The trees surrounding the clearing in the woods were so massive and thick. Their branches were so intertwined that even when the sunlight came pouring down through the gaps between the leaves, it barely reached the ground below. The water flowing under the falls created soft cascades of water, creating a nice rhythm in the background.

It was silent aside from the faint sound of the falling drops of water and wind, and it actually smelled like nature, a subtle perfume mixed with the fresh spring breeze.

After some time, Blair opened her eyes to finally turn her attention to the person sitting behind her who was currently leaning forward against the edge of the tree trunk. Her gaze met his amused eyes.

"I am impressed," he commented, breaking the silence. "This is a very lovely place. How did you discover this place?" he asked curiously.

"Been exploring." Blair shrugged. "Sure you don't want to loosen up a bit?" Blair asked, looking suggestively at Alpha Silas.

He looked back at her and then back into the forest, before returning his eyes to hers.

"If you insist," he replied simply, standing up straight.

He walked to stand beside her, he let the coat he had over him fall to the grass.

The cool breeze blew by, causing some leaves to brush past his body.

Alpha Sila's eyes began flickering gold, as his claws and canines began elongating, while black furs started sprouting from his entire body. He then crouched down as his bones kept reshaping and reforming, as he shifted into his huge, magnificent black wolf, with glowing golden eyes.

"Beautiful," Blair said in awe, as she slowly approached him.

Alpha Silas watched as she drew nearer. His amber eyes fixed on hers intently. He held her stare.

Blair stopped just short of him and looked at him from head to toe before saying, "You are quite spectacular, too."

The evening sun ray illuminated the dark red glow in his eyes, making it seem darker and more dangerous than usual.

Blair's heart raced fast. Her breathing grew heavy and shallow, as she slowly stretched her hand out to stroke his fur.

Without warning, Alpha Silas suddenly lunged towards her and pinned her to the ground, as she giggled and playfully struggled underneath him.

He lowered his head over her throat, nuzzling it gently. She arched her neck upwards, letting him explore the soft skin underneath.

Her fingers brushed against the rough fur, as she ran them slowly through his head.

She breathed deeply and softly, enjoying every inch of contact she could get with the creature that had captured her heart in a friendly way.

Suddenly his tongue darted out and licked her neck. Blair froze, as she felt the tickle of his tongue, along with the slight sting he left behind. She could feel herself shaking underneath the powerful wolf.

"Alpha Silas!" She protested breathlessly.

She tried desperately to wriggle free of his grip, but he wouldn't relent, keeping his firm hold on her.

He nuzzled her, moving back and indicating she climbed his back. She did so and wrapped her arms around his neck tightly.

He immediately stood up and took off running.

Blair screamed and clung tighter to him, as the chilly air hit her face. But despite that, she couldn't stop laughing as he kept running deeper into the woods.

Alpha Silas had never let anyone ride his wolf, not until her.

He enjoyed every second of being able to show her all this side of him. He loved seeing her laugh. He loved how her eyes lit up. He loved how beautiful she was. But even more than that, he loved hearing her laughter. He always wanted to hear it again.

Alpha Silas couldn't understand what was happening to him, why he felt so strongly for Blair.

While still in his train of thought, all of a sudden, Alpha Silas's wolf felt a sharp piercing pain by his side, causing him to stumble a bit.

"Alpha!" Blair yelled out, frightened, as the wolf began staggering.

Alpha Silas's vision started becoming blurry. He heard Blair's screams before everything faded away into darkness.

Chapter Ten

Blair groaned in pain as she felt the coldness of the concrete floor against her bruised body.

Her head pounded painfully with a dull ache that throbbed all the way to the tips of her chained hands.

She squeezed her eyes tight shut as tears welled up within them and spilled over onto her cheeks.

She had been strong for so long, refusing to give in.

She tried desperately to focus on the warm smell in the air, but it was impossible to ignore the icy chill that still seeped through her clothing from being in the dark, cold dungeon for what must have been hours.

The sound of heavy chains rattled along the stone walls around her as someone entered, a fire torch flickering in front of her face.

The light grew brighter until it illuminated her surroundings.

She blinked away the spots that danced in her eyes and squinted upward at her captors. "You're going to need more torches after this," she commented. Her voice sounded hoarse and strained, like she hadn't spoken properly in days, but the man above her paid her no attention.

"If it isn't the infamous Cadence." The stalker, whose face was still hidden from the light, laughed out. "It took you long enough, you know."

She knew what it was already.

"What do you want?" Blair growled, though her patience was wearing thin quickly. "This is getting old."

The stalker didn't respond, only stepped forward with the lit torch and began shining it directly into her eyes.

Blair winced from the painful intensity of the bright beam.

"I see you got yourself a little boyfriend," the stalker said with a smirk, his voice tinged with mockery. "Does he know you're a thousand years older? Does he know you're the Cadence he has been searching for?" he chuckled, seeing the guilty look on Cadence's face.

"Oh! He doesn't. Isn't that sad." He shook his head in mock sadness.

"How pitiful." He paused. "I wonder how he'll take it once he learns about who you truly are, and the fact you've been lying to him all the while. What name did you give yourself again? Blair, it is right. Poor woofy woofy," he tooted.

"Shut up," Blair spat back, trying to keep her cool. She didn't want to give him the satisfaction of getting to her.

Her throat burned uncomfortably, making it hard to breathe.

He leaned forward until his face was mere inches away from hers. "I can make this all go away. I can stop your pain and restore all you lost centuries ago. Bring your power and name back. Make you the goddess you once were. All you have to do is join us to destroy the werewolves." His grin became feral and cruel when she failed to react to his proposition.

He reached out and placed a hand on her arm.

Pain shot through her muscles, paralyzing her limbs, where they were restrained at her sides.

She tried to scream, to scream her rage and defiance of this horrible creature who had dared to touch her, but it came out more of a strangled whimper instead.

His hand was burning against her skin with an unbearable heat, and a wave of nausea washed over her.

"All you have to do is say yes," he said slowly and clearly.

She looked at him helplessly, unable to move or speak despite the intense heat.

"Say yes, Cadence," he said softly, reaching out and wiping her brow with a cloth that smelled foul. "You know I will never harm you if you do this one thing for me, right? I am asking you this only because you mean so much to me, and I would hate to see my favorite goddess suffer from such misery. It's just such a shame, really, that you were never destined to be anything other than perfect.

I guess we all have our bad breaks. No one deserves the pain you've gone through for thousands of years. You deserve to live better. Why don't you consider doing that? Just join us. You'll never be alone again. And you won't be alone forever... I promise."

"You talk so much for a male," Cadence spat, glaring angrily at him from beneath her eyelids.

She was trembling with rage, her body trembling so violently it took every ounce of strength not to rip apart her bonds.

The stalker seemed surprised by her response. "Well, you seem awfully angry for someone who knows you'll never escape." He raised an eyebrow, his smirk widening into something sinister. "Is it because you think your precious wolf would come save you?"

Her eyes flashed silver as she snarled out her answer. "Leave Silas out of this!"

Her voice echoed off the cold walls, reverberating in her ears and echoing against her brain.

For a moment, silence filled the room, and then the stalker chuckled. "So you really care for him. How cute."

Then, suddenly, the smile faded, and he looked furious. "But you have no idea what I'm capable of, do you, Cadence?" His words trailed off ominously. "I can get rid of you easily, and that will make all the difference. And also, I can show you what true freedom feels like, and you'll never want to return to that wretched life again." His smile returned to its normal, cheerful state. "Or we can play another game. One I'm sure you have heard before."

His hand slipped from her arm, but he did not remove it completely. Instead, his large hand gently brushed a lock of hair from her forehead, caressing her skin softly, reverently. Then he pulled away abruptly, his expression hardening into a sneer. "Let's begin the game, shall we?" he said, looking down upon her with amusement. "Your time begins now, Cadence. Choose where you stand. Tik tok Cadence," he said, trailing a finger on her face, but she pulled back immediately.

"Ahh, you're quite feisty for someone in chains. But you will learn to love my kindness someday." He smiled, releasing her face and allowing his hand to fall limply to his side.

"You're such a coward," Blair said calmly, watching his every movement. "I mean, are you so scared of what I can do to you? Is that why you have the antimagic chains on me? You're a moon stalker, you should do better," Blair said, hoping he would take the bait.

The man scowled, a deep rumble rising in his chest. "Don't toy with me, woman. Your little tactic won't work on me." The darkness in his eyes was obvious, but Blair didn't shake.

She stared at him, unflinching, and let her gaze linger on his piercing eyes. She couldn't allow herself to surrender this quickly. Not without trying everything possible to free herself first. She would fight him tooth and nail, if needed, for Silas's sake. If nothing else, she would ensure he suffered a painful death once she was free.

He chuckled darkly. "Do you really expect me to fall for that?" he asked, his voice low and threatening.

"That's the idea," she smirked. She watched him carefully, ready to act if things went wrong. She could feel her magic churning inside her, preparing for the battle to come. She could feel the familiar hum of the spell coursing through her veins, her heart beating loudly against her ribcage. But there was nothing more she wanted than to see him fall before her before it inevitably happened.

"Let me watch you try," the stalker said with a knowing smile playing on his lips.

She saw red.

She felt her anger boiling inside her chest, the fire licking her insides and demanding release.

In a single swift motion, she twisted her arms still in her bindings and maneuvered her hands to grab hold of the stalker's wrist, which rested in between her cell rails and squeezed tightly, causing him to cry out in agony, as she pulled him closer.

With great force, she swung her fist back and punched him in the nose. His head snapped to the side sharply, and he stumbled backward.

"That's for hurting Silas!"

The sound of breaking bones filled her ears as soon as she had released her grip, but she hardly noticed.

The man cursed under his breath, grabbing at his now bloodied nose. "Damn bitch. You shouldn't have done that."

He growled menacingly, stalking towards her, as the pain started to subside from his nose, leaving behind a trail of crimson across his face.

He pulled open the cell door, letting himself in, while Blair stalked backward.

"I will crush your skull. I will break you. I swear it! You will pay for your insolence." He threatened her, raising his clenched fist as if to hit her.

She narrowed her eyes at him. "Good luck trying. I'd rather take my chances with the other wolves."

"You are foolish. I will kill you before I lose sight of the goal I set for myself. It's too easy to forget. These creatures don't understand what it means to truly be powerful. To be revered above others. They are weak and pathetic, and so are you, as you've become just like them!" The stalker growled out each word as he advanced toward her.

Blair backed up further until she collided with the wall behind her. There she stood, waiting. She was willing to go through whatever he had in for her. All she knew was she still wasn't going to spill or join them.

"I'll show you how weak you are," the stalker whispered menacingly.

He drew back his hand again, and a small dagger appeared in his palm, flashing dangerously bright with magic in the flickering light. The blade glinted wickedly. "Now you listen, Cadence..." he paused, taking a moment to study her reaction to his words.

"This will be your first time torture. I hope it hurts."

He lunged for her.

And for one second, Blair was scared. Terrified.

But she was determined to remain strong, to show him that she would never succumb. That he couldn't hurt her, no matter how much he might want to.

The moment passed quickly, as the knife came flying toward her face, but instead of dodging or avoiding her attacker's attack, she closed her eyes and waited patiently.

The knife slammed into her shoulder, and she felt the impact resonate throughout her entire being.

Blair gasped in pain, dropping to the floor and gripping her wound. Blood gushed through her fingers, dripping onto the ground as she clutched her injured shoulder. She opened her eyes slowly, turning her gaze downward, looking at her bloodied hand and at the blood-soaked rips in her blouse, the hole tore through the center where the knife struck her skin. Her eyes widened, and she began crying. Her vision blurred slightly as tears started to stream down her cheeks.

"Why? Why would you do this?" She sobbed, shaking her head helplessly, unable to comprehend why anyone would harm her.

The stalker grinned maliciously at her, his eyes gleaming maliciously in the dim light.

"To teach you a lesson."

He raised the dagger right above her injured shoulder

"One last Cadence. Join us now against the werewolves. And in return, I'll give you everything you lost and more. I'll teach you how to be powerful, how to protect those you cherish."

She shook her head furiously, tears streaming down her cheeks, but refused to accept the reality of what was happening.

"No! Don't do this. Please. You can't do this. I..." Blair pleaded for the first time, as the pain shot up in an excruciating manner.

The stalker laughed mockingly and threw the dagger aside and let his fist connect to her head, sending her flying forward.

Her face landed heavily against the stone floor. The wind knocked from her lungs, her body trembling uncontrollably. The world spun around her, spinning dizzily, and her vision blurred. Her ears rang painfully, filling her senses with a loud tingling sensation, and in no time, she blacked out.

Chapter Eleven

Alpha Silas woke up with a groan, tossing and turning, as his eyes slowly fluttered open.

All he saw was white.

"Where the fuck am I?" He jolted upright to a sitting position, causing a sharp migraine to hit the back of his head.

"Easy Alpha." He heard the pack doctor rush to him.

"Why am I here?" Alpha Silas asked, bewildered, still trying to gain his recollection from before now.

"You were attacked in the woods, Alpha," the doctor explained, trying to fix the machines the Alpha was connected to.

"You were injected with a certain substance that contained loads of wolfsbane and coated with silver, which caused severe internal damage, and you've been out for the past few days."

"What the hell happened?" Alpha Silas tried again, feeling his brain starting to piece together.

He was in the woods? Doing what exactly? He pondered as fragments of images tried to form in his head.

The doctor shook her head sadly, "The amnesia only lasts for a few minutes, it'll wear off soon." She paused, taking note of how much pain Alpha Silas's expression was displaying.

"Woods..." he muttered, and just like a light switch turned on in his brain, he suddenly remembered.

"Blair! Where's she at? We were together in the woods? Where is she now!" Alpha Silas growled, almost pulling off the syringe in him.

"Please calm down Alpha," the doctor pleaded. "You're still not in the right state to react deeply."

"She was taken." Another voice came through the door, and Alpha Silas looked up with a bewildered expression, not believing his eyes.

"Lubo?" Alpha Silas asked, looking at the large man who had just stepped through the door.

"Alpha Silas," Lubo answered solemnly as he made his way from the door, further inside revealing Otsana, who had a guilty look on her face.

"Otsana?" Alpha Silas called out, shocked she was there too.

"Alpha Silas," she said with a guilty smile, walking to his bedside alongside.

"I'm sorry I flared up that way, and we left," she apologized.

"Mhm." Alpha Silas nodded.

"We are really sorry, mate," Lubo said, patting the Alpha on his shoulder.

"Where is Blair?" Alpha Silas asked, noticing the awkward look on their faces.

"They took her away," Otsana finally replied sadly.

Alpha Silas furrowed his brow, "What do you mean they? Who did? What does that even mean!" he was growing angry now, but it didn't seem to matter.

"Alpha Silas, please calm down." The Doctor urged.

"Where did they take her!" He growled at them all.

Lubo and Otsana shared a hesitant glance, then Otsana spoke. "We really don't know. We found you almost half dead in the woods, bleeding out, unconscious."

"How did you know I was there?" Alpha Silas asked curiously. "Cause no one knows there. It was more like a safe haven for her."

"Before you completely passed out, your wolf sent a message to your beta, giving him your location, and beta James immediately reached out to us, and we rushed there, retrieving you," Otsana explained.

That wasn't very helpful at all. "Well, where is she now?!"

"We don't know," Lubo said truthfully. "But there was a note beside you when we found you. Your beta has it." As though on cue, beta James swiftly walked in.

"Alpha," Beta James said, moving close to his bed.

Alpha Silas was content with his presence and felt an odd sense of familiarity come over him as Beta James placed a small piece of paper next to him.

Beta James stood back respectfully and waited for a reaction. Alpha Silas picked up the folded piece of paper, unrolling it carefully.

As he skimmed the contents of the note, the blood drained from his face, and his jaw clenched painfully tight. He let his gaze fall on the page, and his anger started to burn brightly in his eyes.

"You said you found it beside me right?" Alpha Silas asked once again. His voice was quiet but steady, laced with fury.

"Yes alpha," Beta James responded, still watching silently.

"The moon stalkers have her," he said with gritted teeth.

Beta James gave no indication of being surprised by this news at all, his eyes never wavering from Alpha Silas' face as he remained silent, awaiting Alpha Silas' instructions.

"Get ready Beta, we are going to get her," he ordered quietly, still glaring furiously at the note in front of him.

Beta James nodded in understanding, and quickly left without another word. Alpha Silas sighed heavily, closing his eyes briefly before forcing himself to turn his attention back to the note.

"We can still help, you know," Otsana said, breaking the tense silence.

"Otsana offering to help? Tell me a better joke." Alpha Silas scoffed darkly, his attention still on the note before him.

"I admit that I've been difficult, and we started on a rough part. I'm really sorry, and to Blair, do you realize that she saved us all too? I owe it to her," she argued, her voice pleading.

"Oh yes, she's the hero here. Of course, she does." Alpha Silas shot back sarcastically.

"Because she's always been so damn selfless, unlike some people I know," he said with a sneer.

"Kill me already." Otsana rolled her eyes.

"And why would I do that? You're such a fucking nuisance," Alpha Silas spat angrily.

"So you want me to leave?" Otsana asked incredulously. "This whole time, I've been telling myself to try and keep it sane, but you're pushing the buttons."

"If you think I'm going to sit here and listen to you bitch about your 'all of a sudden selflessness', then you're sorely mistaken Otsana. There are better things to worry about." Alpha Silas rolled his eyes.

"And there we go again," Lubo said with a sigh, falling back on a nearby chair, while Otsana and Alpha Silas kept bickering.

"You both should get married and kiss already," Lubo said.

"Ewww!" Otsana and Alpha Silas echoed together, turning over to Lubo with a disgusted face.

"Finally, we are back. What's the next plan Alpha?" Lubo said immediately.

"We find the bastards that took Blair captive," Alpha Silas said, his voice serious and stern, the look in his eyes showing how important this mission was to him.

"Then let's do it," Lubo said, looking at Alpha Silas expectantly.

Alpha Silas quickly got to his feet, forgetting he was connected to a syringe.

"Oww." Alpha Silas winced in the sharp pain that came with it.

"Careful!" The doctor, who had been observing silently, exclaimed, rushing to his side, as he staggered a bit.

"I feel lightheaded," Alpha Silas said as the doctor helped him back to the bed.

"The drug still has an effect on you, plus the motion at which you got up was too quick," the doctor explained, "I'm sorry Alpha, but you'll need to rest in for a bit longer before you can exert any form of energy."

"Rest?" Alpha Silas snorted bitterly, his voice dripping with sarcasm. "Where is the time?!"

"I'm sorry Alpha, but if I let you go now, your wolf would be greatly affected. The wolfsbane weakened it, but it'll be stable soon enough."

The doctor said, making Alpha Silas realize he hadn't reached out to Leo since he woke up.

He tried to concentrate, reaching out to Leo, but all he got was a faint response from his wolf.

"How much rest do I need?" Alpha Silas asked, praying to the moon goddess that it doesn't exceed an hour's time, because he was eager to get to Blair in no time.

"Three days." The doctor deadpanned.

"Fuck! No."

***

"I think we should pitch a tent here. It'll soon be nightfall," Lubo said as he fell to the ground, leaning his back on the large trunk behind him.

"Alright." Alpha Silas agreed, sitting cross-legged and resting the back of his head against the trunk next to Lubo.

After the three days' rest, Alpha Silas felt better. But he needed his strength to save Blair.

The rest of the team, which included Beta James and Otsana, sat on a fallen log across them.

All were tired and exhausted, not having slept well for the past few days. They've been on the journey to find the moon stalkers' hideout and rescue Blair.

Suddenly Alpha Silas noticed something in the distance, something unusual in its shape. At first, he thought it could be a tree, but realized that it wasn't, but rather, it seemed like a person dressed all in white, standing in the center of a clearing.

"Someone's following us," Alpha Silas pointed out. He was surprised at how calm he sounded compared to how angry he was feeling inside.

"Let me take care of it," Beta James said, getting to his feet.

"No, I'll do it myself," the Alpha said, getting to his feet.

"But you're just-"

"I'm okay James!" the Alpha exclaimed, walking towards the direction the figure cited.

"I mean, we could all go check it out, rather than talk about who'd go first," Otsana said, getting to her feet, trailing after the alpha

"You guys stay here and wait for my signal," he commanded, stopping the rest from following him any further.

"Keep your voices low, and stay hidden. Don't make a single sound until I give you the signal. Do not approach unless I say otherwise. Got it?"

Both Otsana and Lubo nodded.

With that, Alpha Silas continued walking toward his destination, watching the unmoving figure with keen eyes.

When he arrived at the spot where the figure stood, his eyes widened, and shock flooded through his entire body. He knew that silhouette anywhere; it was Blair. And it looked as though someone had taken a knife to her beautiful face.

Blood covered her skin along with dried tear tracks. Her clothes hung limply off her body, showing that her captors had stripped her, leaving only her underwear and bra, the material covering her chest and arms as they lay uselessly over her body.

"Blair!" He yelled out, rushing to grab her, just to grasp the air.

There was nothing but empty space there.

"Shit." He breathed, shaking his head in disbelief as he looked around desperately.

Was he hallucinating?

"Shit. Fuck. Shit!"

His eyes were scanning the area frantically, trying desperately to see if he could locate the source of her disappearance.

His heart thudded loudly in his ears, and he shook his head frantically, searching for her.

"Dammit." He growled under his breath angrily, trying to get calm as he felt Leo at the surface.

He turned around slowly to see a strange creature, which looked human but had something eerie about it.

He didn't know if it was the piercing eyes or the long, pointed elf-like ears, or the ridiculous more than 6ft, causing Alpha to look up at his towering height.

"What are you?" Alpha Silas asked.

"That shouldn't be what you should be asking, don't you think?" The strange creature said as he began pacing with his hand behind his back. "The question should be, where is Cadence, or do I say, Blair?"

"What do you mean?" Alpha Silas asked, totally lost. "Cadence isn't Blair," he defended.

"Oh, what do you know?" The creature laughed heartily.

"The soul which you searched for was right beside you the whole while," the creature said.

Alpha Silas didn't know if he should be pissed or relieved that he finally found Cadence at long last, only that she had been the one who had helped them.

He now understood the reason for her kind gesture and hospitality.

He felt betrayed.

"Where is she?" he asked, his voice sounding more like a growl than he would have liked it to.

"I'm afraid I cannot tell you that, Alpha," the creature said with a shrug.

"But what I can tell you is, the one you are searching for is she who can save you," the creature said and disappeared into thin air before Alpha Silas could utter another word.

"What just happened?" Otsana asked, coming up behind him, others joining them.

"Blair is the Cadence that we have been searching for."

Chapter Twelve

Blair woke up to a stinging pain in her jaw.

Someone had knocked her out the painful way. Looking around her, she grimaced.

She was sitting on a cold concrete floor in a different filthy room, with barely any light.

Barely five feet high, the walls were made of strong tars with a tiny window that hardly gave any light.

There was a great iron door that was locked from the outside.

The ceiling, if it could be called that, sloped downwards from the door. The area around the door could have been up to seven feet, but when it came to the wall she was chained to, it was a mere five feet.

The door had a small hole which she could peek out from, but she couldn't summon the energy to stand up, let alone walk to the door.

Looking out the window, she tried to figure out what time of the day it was and how long she had been there.

The light from the window didn't look too bright.

Maybe because it was dusk?

It could even be mid-day, depending on the location of the window.

She had no idea what time it was or where she could be, and the thought of being alone in an unknown place drained the last of her energy.

Lifting her hands to rub her stinging jaw, she discovered she couldn't.

Her hands had been chained to the wall. And so had her legs.

Damn it!

They should at least have left room for her to reach her face.

She felt the tears well up in her eyes and swallowed. She would not give them the satisfaction of crying. She could not panic, or else they would win. She needed to stay strong. But she was weak. So weak.

She had not had anything to eat since the previous evening when she'd eaten with Alpha Silas and his friends.

Where was he?

Had they killed him?

They must have shot him with some pretty powerful stuff because he'd fallen immediately, not even stirring when they had taken her away kicking and screaming.

She heard footsteps approaching and pretended to be asleep.

Soon the footsteps stopped in front of her door, and she heard a key being inserted into the lock. The door was thrown open, and two males walked in. Her eyes were closed, but she could sense them.

"She is still unconscious. Bring water," one of them ordered.

Silently, Blair thanked the moon goddess. Her throat was parched, and it would be a blessing to get a drop of water on her lips.

Still pretending to be unconscious, she waited eagerly for the water to arrive.

Soon, an extra set of footsteps approached the dungeon, and a blast of cold water slapped her face and body.

Shrieking like a wounded cat, she shied away from them, totally abandoning her plan to lock the water.

The water was dirty and smelly, like a fishmonger's bath water that had been kept for two weeks.

They laughed as she coughed and sputtered, trying to draw a clean breath.

"That was quite an awakening, no?" the one who seemed to be the second in command asked her.

He was tall and thick, like a well-built tree trunk, with sandy brown hair and lifeless black eyes that put the fear of death into her body.

The other two were quite alike. Though not quite as tall as the second in command, they were still of threatening height and had smooth round features that could almost be considered handsome. One was paler than the other, and that was the only difference.

Shivering with more than just cold, she shifted to the other end of the cramped dungeon.

"No need to run, there's no way out Cadence."

Blair wasn't surprised anymore...

She knew that they knew her true identity.

"What do you want from me?" She knew what they wanted and was quite surprised that they still kept her alive till this time.

Their leader laughed while the others smirked.

"Like you don't know."

"If I knew, I wouldn't be asking," she snapped, purposely

After staring at her for a few seconds, they realized she was serious and frowned.

"You are Cadence, the great and powerful witch who existed one thousand years ago, are you not?"

Blair scoffed.

"You think you can confirm my identity only now? Idiots!"

The paler one took a threatening step forward.

"How dare you?"

Refusing to be daunted, Blair lifted her chin and eyed him. "If you take one more step, I will turn you into a dwarf with two noses and a lizard's tail."

She knew her powers were restrained by their master, but she just had to try, and to her happiness, he seemed to believe her.

The color drained from his face, and he froze, suddenly regarding her with new eyes.

Blair tried to disguise her glee.

Good for the mulish brute.

She turned back to the second in command with renewed confidence.

"I ask again, what do you want from me?"

He observed her quietly for a few seconds before answering.

"At the very least, don't interfere in our battle with the werewolves like you did the last time."

The moon stalkers, the perpetual enemies of the werewolves, she thought, with an internal eye roll.

"I will decide which battle to interfere in without your advice."

How dare they try to give her orders!

Why, if she had her full powers, she would have turned them into ugly mice.

"But the wolves are your enemies too," one noted, reminding her.

"I have no enemies except those who look for war when there should be peace," she replied boldly.

"The werewolves have done nothing to wrong you. Why won't you let them be?"

The second in command which she had noted to be a dumbass at this point, was clearly at a loss.

"We only implore you to help us get rid of them. Are they, not your enemies too? Let us help each other."

"I will not."

He sighed and eyed the sword that seemed glued to his body.

Then I'm afraid I will have to do this."

She was just about to ask what he wanted doing, before deciding against it.

It was certainly not going to be something good.

Gathering the last of her energy, she tried casting a spell for the umpteenth time to get the chains off her.

To her utmost surprise, it worked, and the shackles fell noisily to the ground.

The moon stalkers stared at her dumbfounded, and she smiled unbelievably.

They, including her, hadn't seen that coming.

Still too weak to make a run for it, she sat there smirking at them.

Finally, the second in command snapped out of his shocked trance and called for the binder he had prepared.

Binder?

What binder?

Panic seized her and propelled her into action.

She did not have enough power to teleport, but she could definitely cloak herself to make them think she had disappeared.

Mouthing the words, Blair closed her eyes and started the spell.

She felt the power take over her and start to cover her with bright light. Then suddenly, the darkness descended again, and she felt the weight of shackles on her hands and feet once more.

Opening her eyes, she stared foolishly at her chained limbs, not understanding how they had come to be there.

She looked up at the smiling face of the second in command...

"I bet you didn't see that one coming."

Indeed she had not.

"They said you used to have very enlightening dreams. I guess this was excluded from it. Maybe as punishment for supporting the werewolves?"

They dissolved in fits of laughter.

Blair ignored them and closed her eyes, preparing to cast another spell.

She started chanting the words and felt the familiar rise of power, but it suddenly bounced back like someone or something had pushed it back.

She opened her eyes and stared at them in horror as the meaning of the 'binder' he had prepared occurred to her.

It was a magical binder, unlike the previous one, which was to restrain her magic to some point. This was fashioned to completely drain her magic!

"What have you done?" She screeched.

"I learned that trick from a hybrid witch. You have to admit it is very useful."

"You misbegotten bastards."

Walking up to her, he bent to her level and withdrew a small sharp knife from the side of his trousers. Admiring the blade, he placed it against her neck and pushed it.

The blade bit into her skin and brought out a gasp from her.

"Will you fight on our side or on that of the werewolves?" he asked angrily

"I will not fight for you losers."

The second in command lifted the knife away from her neck and brought the back of it down on her arm.

Pain tore through her arm like lightning as the knife collided with her skin, and the scream she had been trying to hold in burst out.

She held onto her tears like a lifebuoy, clinging to dear life.

She would not cry.

"Will you fight against your natural enemies, the werewolves, or will you be foolish and continue this meaningless stubbornness?" he asked, waving the knife under her nose in glee.

"I would rather rot in here."

She told him boldly, refusing to show any fear.

"You think someone will come for you!" He said with realization.

"So you must have people working for you. Or at least someone."

Blair ignored him and looked in the other direction.

"Who is it?" he demanded hotly.

"Like I would tell you," she murmured

He giggled like a schoolgirl and clapped his hands in glee.

"By the hair of the moon goddess, it's the werewolf Alpha. The one we took you from your woofy toy. No wonder you wouldn't betray them and fight with us."

Blair ignored him totally, refusing to give him ammunition to use against her, but the brute didn't give up.

"Please tell me you don't fancy yourself in love with him."

She couldn't help it. She blinked.

Twice!

Oh, skies and seas!!

Now he was really going to have a good laugh.

But he did quite the opposite.

He got mad at her and grabbed her neck, choking her.

Blair struggled to get his hands off her, but considering that she was unable to even touch her jaw, she couldn't reach his hands.

"How dare you let that slime touch you? The likes of him are not fit to kiss the soles of your feet," he told her.

He thought they had slept together?

Oh, if only they had! Then she would die with the memory of his big strong hands on her body.

And this brute thought he was the one worthy of her?

What a very inflated opinion of himself he had.

Blair tried shaking her head to show that she hadn't slept with him, but apparently, he didn't understand.

Pinning her to the wall, he bent and licked her neck, totally oblivious to the shudders of disgust wracking her body.

When he finally noticed, he mistook it for pleasure and smiled.

"You like it?"

Her head was beginning to spin from lack of oxygen, and even if she had the energy, she wouldn't dare dignify his question with an answer.

Grabbing the front of her dress, he pulled roughly.

"Now I'm going to show you what a real man looks like."

Dread seized the remaining strength Blair had left. She was going to be defiled by this filthy beast? She sent a prayer to the skies and every other deity she could think of.

One of the moon stalkers coughed.

"The overlord asked us not to touch her."

The stalker from the day before.

So who was this pig, huffing and puffing over her? The tears swirled their way down her cheeks, and she let them go helplessly.

Taking a deep breath, presumably to get his 'desire' under control, he stood up and left her, locking the door behind him.

Chapter Thirteen

Silas had lost count of the number of times he had seen it. Every time he closed his eyes, it felt as if they were waiting patiently for him, waiting to pounce on him and strangle him with their claws, and when he was not asleep? They managed to crawl into the deepest of his heart, tugging at it and leaving their trails that were permanent as a stamp.

He was sure he wasn't losing his mind. He knew what he saw, it felt so real, too real to be untrue, but no matter how much he convinced himself, his sanity didn't seem to care. The images would always flash before his eyes, like a bad omen, the moment he closed his eyes and even when he didn't have to.

He had been so exhausted from wanting to make sense of this whole thing that he slept off without even knowing.

It seemed dark at first, but then it got brighter, giving him the perfect view of those men in black, and the familiar woman who was in their midst. Her rich blonde locks looked pale and dusty, her golden skin that had also radiated like fire in the night gave off a faint glow and those warm chocolate brown eyes that had drawn me in since the first time he met her had turned cold and lifeless, reflecting nothing in them. They didn't even blink anymore when she stared back at her captives. She looked like she had been stripped of all her glory and her emotions, she didn't look like she was even aware that he was close. She was nothing like her former self.

The sight broke him.

Leo was threatening to take over inside of Silas, who tried unsuccessfully to keep him at bay, his teeth snarled with vengeance and thirst.

"Soon, boy." Silas assured him quietly as they moved closer, trying to get into a better hiding spot through the pillars that separated us from them. He knew Leo wouldn't hesitate to attack him any minute now. He had never hesitated before.

Silas watched each of them kick her hard against her stomach as they taunted and mocked her, calling her ugly names, saying things about how they would love to see her bleed, to watch how she fell apart under all of that pain. All those words made his blood boil, fury consumed him, and he knew Leo wanted to rip them open, shred them like paper and tear them apart one by one. And Silas let him.

A force sent them flying back to the other side, landing on their backs. It took him a while to find his footing again, to calm himself down from that surge of adrenaline. Once he was able to breathe properly again, he was quick to move his attention to the scene before him. What had just happened?

Cadence let out a soft whimper that sent Silas charging toward the group again with his golden eyes glowing with doom, anarchy and chaos in the dark. He wanted to hurt them so bad that they would beg for mercy. He wanted to make them feel fear, to make them understand how wrong they were for messing with her.

But that force sent Leo and him flying back again, the impact worse than the previous.

Silas groaned once more as he forced himself up, looking around frantically, trying to figure out what just happened. That's when the realization hit him. There was a barrier, an invincible wall that was stopping them.

He tried again, refusing to give up so easily until he ran out of breath. He had never hated himself more than he already did, as he felt puny and useless, and he couldn't do anything about it.

One of the men with strange purple eyes that looked menacing kicked Cadence even harder before he spat on her calling her an "Old slut".

Silas thought of ways to make this man pay, and Leo thought of how his bare heart would feel against his claws.

Silas moved away from the pillar, tiptoeing so he wouldn't attract them. Unfortunately, he stepped on a dried wooden branch that snapped loudly under his weight, enough to gain their attention.

He froze, waiting for them to turn their attention toward him, but they did not, they busied themselves with Cadence like he was not there, and it surprised him.

He raised his hands above his head and waved dramatically, yet they didn't notice him. He moved closer but was stopped by the invincible walls that didn't allow him to get any further. It only meant one thing, they could not see him.

The man with those ethereal purple eyes pulled Cadence by her lush golden locks with so much force that she sobbed loudly as he kept dragging her on the floor with it.

Silas felt his heart break into tiny pieces like shards of glass, sharp and deadly and unforgiving. His anger rose again at the unfairness of it all, but this time he felt helpless as well, and it was the scariest feeling in the world.

The man continued to pull her until they reached a cage where he cuffed her hands to each side of the bars with a wicked grin spreading across his face. He slapped her hard across the face, and his hands lingered shamelessly around her breasts.

Leo couldn't contain his anger.

Cadence spat on the purple-eyed man, which earned her a few slaps and more punches, and that was when Leo lost it.

He sent out a loud soul-piercing roar that echoed around the whole building, making it shake and sending most of the men to their feet, and that was when he woke up panting.

He wasn't in that room anymore. There were no men in black, there was no sign of Cadence, just his endless breathing and the chirping of the birds.

It was one of those dreams. He had found the headquarters of the moon stalkers. He just had to find a way to get in.

And whistling the tune which Lubo had been whistling earlier, Silas strolled out majestically, making it quite an entrance.

There must have been twenty of those bastards waiting for him, but even though his eyes glowed brightly, he played it safe by keeping them busy enough for Otsana and Lubo to free Cadence.

"Hey, they are letting the witch out!" one man yelled.

Shit.

Lubo, who was carrying Cadence, dropped her gently, ready to fight, Otsana didn't back down either, and Silas prayed for a miracle. They circled up on them, and the man with purple eyes charged up to them. Silas punch sent him flying to the wall. Another two were quick to jump on Silas, but he was stronger than they realized and took care of the others easily.

Otsana was fierce, like a wounded lioness, kicking men into walls. She was fighting so bravely, but at some point, it got to her, and Silas could see blood starting to drip from her arm.

They were growing weak, and the number of the moon stalkers increased. They were back in that circle again, and they heard Cadence mumble incoherent words. Smoke filled the air, and everyone coughed with their eyes closed.

When Silas, Lubo and Otsana opened their eyes, they were no longer in the moon stalker's cave, but on a hill. Cadence mumbled a few more words before she lost consciousness.

Chapter Fifteen

It was a quiet dusk as the werewolves of the silver claw clan, led by Alpha Silas, alongside the rogues, prepared for the war that would change their lives.

They were not certain they would win, but they had no other choice but to fight, and they would do so with pride.

As they worked with cooperation, Alpha Silas watched them and smiled. Despite the uncertainty and Chaos of the past few weeks, the bond was still there, and he was glad.

"We are almost ready, Alpha Silas," his beta, James, reported, pulling him out of his thoughts.

He nodded.

"The moon stalkers will soon be here. Make sure everything and everyone is in position."

"Including Cadence?" he enquired quietly. The alpha was very fond of the witch, and he was not ready to get on his bad side.

"Is she awake?"

Beta James shook his head. "She is still resting." Alpha Silas nodded again.

She deserved her rest, considering the amount of energy she had expended in teleporting them from the dungeon they had found her in.

He didn't want to remember the despair he had walked around with when he'd been unable to find her. She was safe now, and that was all that mattered.

"Then let her rest," he told his beta. "She can sit this one   out."

"Yes Alpha Silas," he responded and followed him inside to prepare their minds for the upcoming battle.

***

Cadence woke up to the calm before a tsunami. She definitely felt refreshed after her reasonably long nap, but she could use a bit more rest.

Staggering from her bed, or rather Silas's bed because she was in his home, she clutched the wall for balance till the house stopped spinning before making her   way   outside.

She must have slept for quite a while because they were prepared for war.

Or maybe they had prepared really fast.

They were fighting with everything in them.

There was every kind of weapon ranging from poisoned arrows and darts, to guns and even swords.

Indeed Alpha Silas was a great leader and a master planner   too.

Speaking of which, where was he?

She hadn't seen him since she had come out. Looking around, she started walking towards the middle of the courtyard when she felt him.

Yes, she felt him before she saw him.

That special link between them had not been broken. And no matter how depleted her powers were, she could still feel him.

He was on the right-hand side of the courtyard, standing by the sycamore tree and talking to James, seemingly oblivious to the thousands of werewolves poised in mid-attack. She called out to him in her mind hoping that he would hear when the first set of moon stalkers attacked.

The werewolves defeated them easily. Some shifted into their wolf form, while some were still in their human form, using the darts and poisoned arrows, having the upper hand.

Just as they did, the next set of moon stalkers poured in, in their numbers, unexpectedly, and soon the tides turned.

Werewolves fell like fruit seeds to the ground at an alarming rate.

Cadence began to fear that they might have lost the battle.

Silas and the wolves were fighting with all their might, but then, so were the moon stalkers.

There were dead bodies all over the ground, and blood was not scarce.

The battle was long and bloody, refusing to end even when there were only ten wolves standing.

Nodding to themselves, the wolves dug into their boots and produced more poisoned darts which they proceeded to use in wounding the moon stalkers.

Alpha Silas shifted to his black ferial wolf, teeth sharp, claws extended, his golden color orbs glared fiercely at their enemies, as Leo was more than ready to tear them limb by limb, till there was nothing left of them.

The wolves followed suit, shifting into their beastly forms.

Alpha Silas roared as he charged a pack of moon stalkers,

snapping his jaws. The alpha's power was immense, even as a wolf, but it wasn't enough for these monsters.

Their speed and endurance outpaced even their wolfish bodies. They had no difficulty killing a werewolf.

His eyes widened when he realized he underestimated the number of these creatures.

Alpha Silas growled as another werewolf was killed by a werewolf hunter within about four minutes of a fierce battle between them.

There were too many.

He had underestimated how many there were.

He had never seen so many in one place before.

But they weren't stopping, not until they were completely annihilated. His head whipped left to right as he scanned the battlefield, watching his enemies fall before his very eyes.

One of them took advantage of his distraction.

Its long tail came whipping around. It hit him in the leg, knocking him off balance, and making him stumble. He snarled at the moon stalker, who snarled back before lunging forward to attack him again.

This time Alpha Silas was ready for the ambush, though. With agility born from years of battle, Alpha Silas leaped up to meet his attackers. One by one, he crushed their skulls, breaking every single jawbone on each one he managed to knock away.

It would have been satisfying if only his injuries hadn't kept slowing him down.

As he dodged attacks thrown his way with great precision, Alpha Silas saw the moon stalkers behind him. He growled loudly, baring his teeth at them. They didn't seem phased by his warning growl. They just kept advancing.

He had to think fast.

He knew he couldn't keep going this way forever. Eventually, he'd run out of energy and would tire faster than he could regenerate his strength, and then they would overwhelm him. Sooner or later.

In his frustration, Alpha Silas let loose a roar, sending a volley of hisses toward the enemy ranks.

The moon stalkers froze.

They stared up at him, shocked, their expressions twisted in fear and uncertainty. The leader finally snapped out of his shock first and growled angrily at him. But before he could launch himself forward, Alpha Silas jumped backward. As soon as he did, the alpha was thrown forward. He crashed hard on his hands and knees, groaning as he tried to stand back up.

His limbs felt weak. He was getting weaker by the minute.

Alpha Silas was able to catch his breath. If he wanted to survive this night, he had to keep up his stamina. Otherwise, it wouldn't matter what kind of shape he was in. The moon stalkers would finish him off. And if he died tonight, the moon stalkers would slaughter everyone. Including his family. His pack.

That thought terrified Alpha Silas. He knew it wasn't a good idea to be afraid when dealing with a bunch of predators who could kill you at any given moment if they wanted to. But being a werewolf always meant being on alert, and it was inevitable that you'd be a target when you lived outside of your territory.

Cadence suddenly came to his rescue unexpectedly, creating a sort of barrier which slowed down the moon stalkers and gave the werewolves renewed vigor to carry on with the fight.

The tide once again started turning against the moon stalkers.

Alpha Silas stood tall and proud with a grim determination. With renewed strength, he attacked. This time, he used both his claws and teeth as weapons in combination with his powerful paws. He bit the necks of the moon stalkers who dared approach him and ripped them to pieces with ease. He tore open flesh, blood splashing everywhere.

The werewolves fought like wild animals, claws and fangs clashed together.

The moon stalkers fought back just as savagely as the werewolves.

Even though they outnumbered the werewolves, Alpha Silas felt more confident than ever that he, and his pack, would win this battle, especially with the help of Cadence, who was a great help in slowing down and immobilizing the moon stalkers.

When he was certain of it, he let out a mighty howl. A howl that shook the trees, vibrating the very air with its volume and its power. When it finished, he stood proud and triumphant and watched, in satisfaction, as the last of the moon stalkers dropped to the ground, dead.

He looked towards Cadence and gave her the biggest smile, showing she had been right. Her expression showed that she knew it, and she returned his smile proudly. She nodded, confirming her confidence. She was right. Everything was going to be alright now. He had won.

She then called out to his pack and said, "We did it!" Their cheers and hollers sounded like music to his ears as he walked over to join them.

Once he joined his pack, he was surrounded by their warm arms and welcomed smiles.

Looking around him in wonder at their victory, Alpha Silas started laughing, and soon, the remaining wolves   joined   him.

It had been a bloody war, but they had won.

Finally!

Turning to Cadence, he smiled sweetly at her and motioned her closer. Cadence giggled and flung her hair, flirting with him as she took slow, sure steps towards him.

She noticed the movement from the corner of her eye but didn't get time to warn him.

The moon stalker sank the blade into Alpha Silas's back before either of them could blink.

She took off in a sprint towards Alpha Silas, but the moon stalker was faster, chanting the cloaking spell with a little extra. He twisted the knife and pushed him away. Alpha Silas stumbled away and collapsed to the ground, unable to move a muscle.

Cadence stopped running abruptly, and her mouth opened wide in silent shock. The rest of the pack stopped running too. There was nothing to say after seeing their Alpha, fallen in the middle of the battleground. No words or sounds escaped her.

Just silence.

The silence was deafening.

Cadence felt her heart pounding inside her chest and heard a loud ringing in her ears.

She slowly turned to face the moon stalker with disbelief written across her face.

Alpha Silas's eyes were closed, and he seemed dead to the world. For a moment, she forgot what she was doing and knelt beside him.

Then, slowly, carefully, she placed a gentle hand on his neck and found his pulse, faint and almost nonexistent.

"Alpha Silas," she whispered quietly, hoping he could hear her. She shook his shoulders lightly, calling out to him as well. Still nothing.

Her heart was beating erratically now, tears forming in her eyes as her throat tightened and she choked on her own emotion. She felt hot tears prick her eyes, dripping onto her face. She sniffed but failed to hold back any more tears.

"What did you do to him?!" She yelled at the Moon stalker, who lay beside her, with a sinister smile playing on his lips. Cadence knew at once that it was a special knife made by a witch that the moon stalker had with him. The panic and pain she felt had voices of their own. They tore from her lips with wretched sobs and the rest of her magic, causing the earth to shatter and kiss the earth, and all the remaining moon stalkers were burnt in the light explosion.

The offending stalker, who had stabbed Alpha Silas, had a shard of wood stuck in his stomach.

He was bleeding and dying. She knew he would not last another minute.

She rushed back to Alpha Silas' side, covering the bleeding puncture with her hand, hoping to salvage it somehow, no matter how much it hurt.

She carefully pulled out the dagger from his abdomen, destroying it at a snap of a finger with her magic, before returning her attention to the dying Alpha.

"Hey, Silas. Look at me, please. Don't you dare die on me," she cried out, her hand covered in his blood, which was still seeping out the wound.

Alpha Silas's life force was fading quickly, and she knew there was nothing she could do but hope that he survived it, as her magic was too weak to sustain him.

"Silas…" She trailed off, as tears fell down her cheeks, while she laid her head on his chest, sobbing. "I'm sorry I couldn't protect you. I should have been right beside you. If I'd been here…" Tears continued pouring from her eyes as she hugged the body of the Alpha.

While in the fit of her sobs, Alpha Silas's hand, slowly wrapped around her.

Her cries quieted instantly.

She lifted her head up to see him looking at her with those deep golden brown eyes of his.

"Silas! You're alive!" She called out happily, hugging him, and pulling back to take a look at his wound to see it was closing back on its own and the bleeding had stopped.

"Oh, my goddess! Your wound. It's healing!" She cried out in joy, engulfing him in a hug once more.

His gaze softened, and he looked up at her sadly, reaching up to caress her cheek lovingly.

"Your tears healed and brought me back to life," he said.

She blinked back her tears and leaned into him, pressing her forehead on his in a tender gesture. He cupped her cheek, stroking her skin affectionately with his thumb.

"Don't cry," he murmured gently, trying to sound comforting.

"Don't you ever leave me," she whispered softly, wiping her tears away with her palm.

Alpha Silas gazed fondly at her.

"Mine," he whispered.

The End.

Did you like this book? Then read Forbidden Blood Moon for free

https://dl.bookfunnel.com/j4aehzebwv

The Blood Moon is the Lycan's most powerful night to defeat the elves over an ancient feud built on lies and betrayal.

Elias Moon is the son of the most powerful man in Manhattan and the heir of the Lycan's pack.
Elias has always lived in his father's shadow, looking up to him and trying to make him proud. But when his father pronounces death on every Elf in the city, he must make a stand and stop the senseless genocide.

There's something his father doesn't know: Elias has fallen for an Elf.

Dorothy Mills is not your typical New Yorker. Although she doesn't remember it, she's the lost daughter of the last Elf King.

When Elias comes into her life, things take a dangerous and exciting turn. The two of them have to stop their races from slaughtering each other while trying to understand the relationship brewing between them.

Follow Brook Winter on Facebook:
https://www.facebook.com/author.brookwinter/
Follow Brook Winter on Twitter:
https://twitter.com/BrookWinte57871
Follow Brook Winter on Instagram: *author.brookwinter*